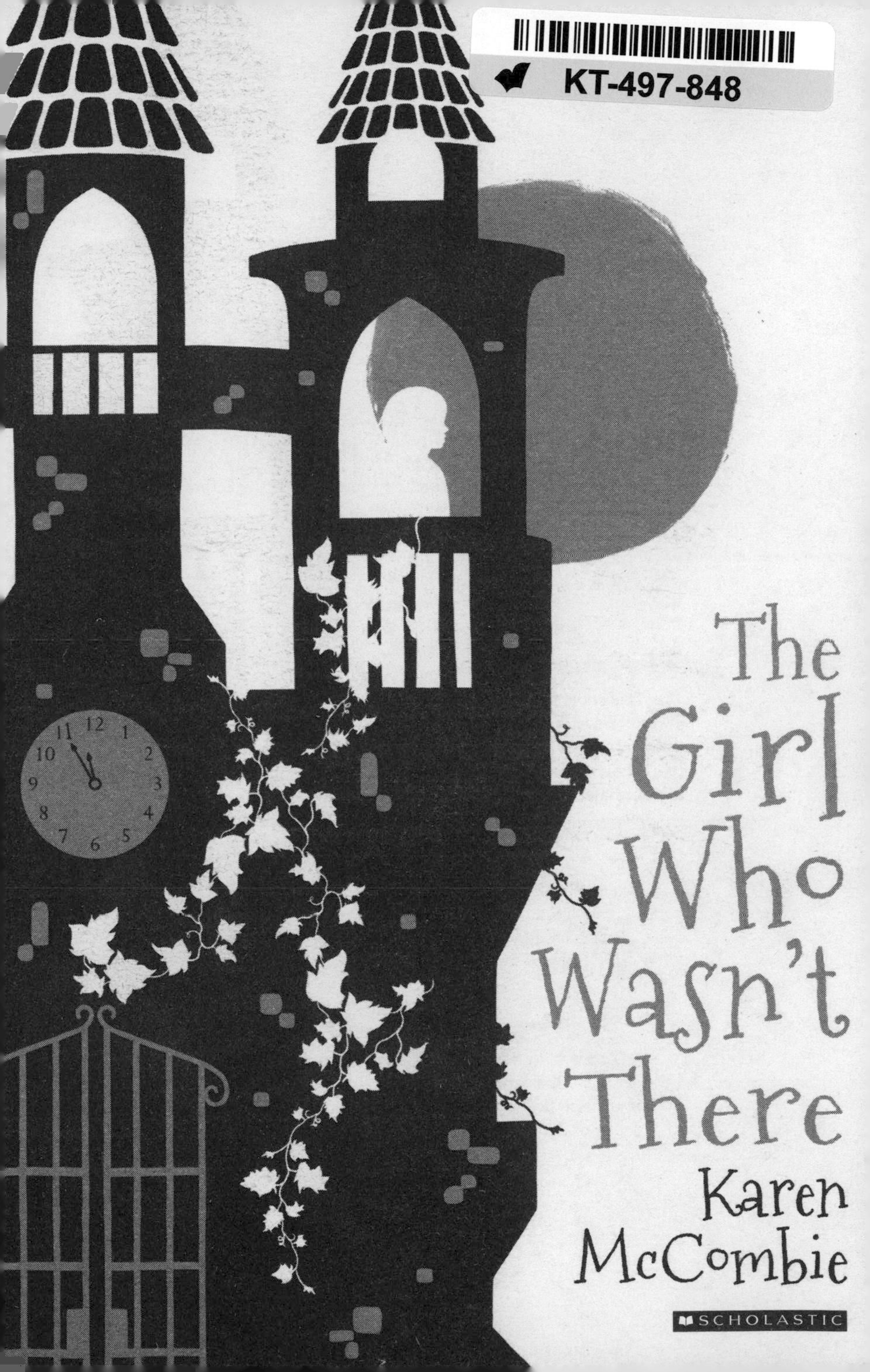

KT-497-848
The Girl Who Wasn't There
Karen McCombie
SCHOLASTIC

Scholastic Children's Books
An imprint of Scholastic Ltd
Euston House, 24 Eversholt Street
London, NW1 1DB, UK
Registered office: Westfield Road, Southam, Warwickshire, CV47 0RA
SCHOLASTIC and associated logos are trademarks and/or
registered trademarks of Scholastic Inc.

First published in the UK by Scholastic Ltd, 2014

Text copyright © Karen McCombie, 2014
The right of Karen McCombie to be identified as the author
of this work has been asserted by her.

ISBN 978 1407 13890 9

A CIP catalogue record for this book
is available from the British Library.

All rights reserved.
This book is sold subject to the condition that it shall not,
by way of trade or otherwise, be lent, hired out or otherwise circulated
in any form of binding or cover other than that in which it is published.
No part of this publication may be reproduced, stored in a retrieval system,
or transmitted in any form or by any means (electronic, mechanical,
photocopying, recording or otherwise) without the prior
written permission of Scholastic Limited.

Printed and bound by CPI Group (UK) Ltd, Croydon, CR0 4YY.

Papers used by Scholastic Children's Books are made
from wood grown in sustainable forests.

1 3 5 7 9 10 8 6 4 2

This is a work of fiction. Names, characters, places,
incidents and dialogues are products of the author's imagination
or are used fictitiously. Any resemblance to actual people,
living or dead, events or locales is entirely coincidental.

www.scholastic.co.uk

With love to Ms Lovegood ... a.k.a. Sami!

Kingston upon Thames Libraries	
KT 2152529 3	
Askews & Holts	17-Oct-2014
JF JF	£6.99
KNJ	KT00000294

R.I.P MY LIFE

The room is bare.

It takes just seconds to see all there is to see.

Sunlight streaming through the curtainless window.

Rose-sprigged Cath Kidston wallpaper, with tiny rips caused by the Blu-tack from my torn-down posters.

Pale laminate on the floor, scuffed where my desk chair once rolled back and forth.

It's so weird; all my life was here, but looking round the emptiness of my bedroom, it's as if it's been snatched away, or as if none of it ever happened, even.

All the laughing (with Lilah and Jasneet, and Saffy too – for a while at least).

All the raging (at Clem, mostly, for pulling those big sister moves, making me feel that small).

All the crying (of rage at Clem; 'cause of my so-called

"friends" flaking out on me; and when Mum died, of course).

"Maisie. . ."

A voice is calling out to me, hazy, faraway.

"Maisie, it's time to go. . ."

The sunlight is so bright it's turned the rectangle of sky in the window a dazzling, peaceful white.

This is the point when I'm meant to feel sad, but strangely, I don't.

I lift my face to the warmth of the white light, feeling floaty, full of calm, full of hope.

It is time; time to close the door on this life and see what happens next.

"Coming," I call out. . .

1 From Me To You Thoughts from your mum, for my darling girls. . .

Wow, I'm *cringing* at myself.

What I wrote in the notebook – "R.I.P. my life" – it makes me sound so pretentious and dramatic.

Or like I'm *dead* or something.

I'm not usually so pretentious and dramatic.

(And I'm definitely not dead.)

But leaving your childhood home can rattle you, I guess.

Packing up thirteen years of yourself into cardboard boxes and removal vans can leave you feeling pretty sentimental.

Still, it's been just half an hour since we left 12 Park Close (since I wrote that schmaltzy stuff in the back of the notebook) but I'm giddy as anything, excited as a five-year-old version of myself at Christmas time.

Clem isn't.

"You know, the *first* time I saw this house, I didn't like it," she says, staring at the sturdy red-brick cottage in front of us.

"Yep, you made that perfectly clear, sweetheart!" Dad answers cheerfully, as he lurches by her carrying a box marked *Kitchen Stuff*.

"But now. . ." she says, leaning unhelpfully on the tall, metal frame of the gate, "now I realize I *hate* it!"

I want to shout "Get over it!" or "Stop making Dad feel bad!" but we'll just get into a fight and then that'll *really* bother Dad.

So I settle for accidentally-on-purpose barging into her with my own box of stuff from the van.

"Ow!" Clem yells theatrically. "What did you do *that* for, you little—"

"Sorry, didn't see you there," I lie quickly, cutting her off mid-rant while stepping through the front door and heading into the narrow hallway of our new home.

Behind me, I hear Clem muttering darkly as she stomps off out of the iron-work gate in the railings and makes for the hired van parked in the road just outside. Seems like she's finally, reluctantly deciding to lend a hand.

The thing is, I know what's going through Clem's mind.

The Park Close house is pretty modern – built in the 1990s – with these huge windows and sliding glass doors that flood it with light. It's surrounded by matching houses, where loads of Clem's friends live. Park Close is also about a five-minute wander from her sixth-form college.

This house was built in the 1890s, and has a musty smell, since no one's lived in it for a while. The windows are small, making it seem quite twilight-ish inside. It's set in the grounds of Nightingale School, with these old black-painted iron railings separating us from the world beyond. It's also a thirty-minute bus ride away from Clem's sixth-form college ("...which I am NOT moving from, by the way!").

So, yeah, I get all that.

And I *would* sympathize with Clem if she took just one second out of her busy, self-centred schedule to think about how the move affects me and Dad.

For me, it's a chance to start all shiny and new. To forget about old friends who morphed into enemies. To go to a new school where people will just know me for myself. Not Maisie Mills, kid sister of spectacularly gorgeous, spectacularly smart, spectacularly sarcastic Clem, or ex-friend of Lilah and Jasneet after spectacularly falling out with them. . . (Shudder.)

And Dad.

If Clem can't bring herself to think how things've been for *me*, she could at least take a squint at it from Dad's point of view. I mean, you'd think someone who's studying for an A-level in psychology would be able to spot that Dad's smile the last few months never quite hid the panic in his eyes. That he's been doing a lot more of the face-rubbing thing with his hands that he always resorts to when he's stressed.

And since one of Clem's *other* subjects is business studies, you'd reckon she could figure out that big mortgage payments and dwindling redundancy packages don't add up too well.

I know that the offer of site manager's job at Nightingale School got Dad dancing round the living room.

I know, 'cause after he got the news he whirled me around the living room till I felt travel-sick and knocked half the furniture over with my flip-flops.

The fact that a rent-free house came with the job

made it like every birthday, Christmas and Father's Day present rolled into one.

"It's a miracle, Maisie!" he'd said to me, when he found out that live-in accommodation was part of the deal, and that yes, there was a space in Year 8 for me, if I wanted to take it up (yes, please, as soon as possible). Both of us had pretended not to notice Clem screeching her chair back and stomping up the stairs under a darker-than-usual cloud.

"Look – feels like home already, doesn't it?" says Dad now, standing in the doorway of the kitchen.

He's tall and skinny and strong, with a chest the perfect height for laying your head on when everything gets too much. Or when you're happy too.

Dumping my box down on to the gappy, worn floorboards of the hall, I go to him and wrap my arms around the grey cotton of his T-shirt and he hugs me right back.

Feeling his chin rest lightly on my head, I turn to see what he wants me to see. Though I can guess.

And there it is – the first thing to be unpacked – perched on a dusty painted shelf in the empty, old-fashioned kitchen.

A silver-framed photo of a happy family.

A dad with fashionably messy dark hair and a wide, white smile, looking totally in love with his girls, big and small.

In one of his arms he holds a cute, dimpled girl of three, with her brown hair in plaits, gazing straight at the camera.

A bigger girl of eight, with her hair hanging long and straight down her back, has her arms reaching around his waist. She is staring up at him adoringly. He has his hand protectively on the back of her flowery sundress.

The dad is looking over his shoulder, his wide, white smile directed at the mum, who is standing slightly apart from her family, her head tilted back as she laughs, sending a shiny waterfall of fair hair tumbling all the way to her waist.

And how do the current Mills family match up to the ten-year-old version in the picture?

The main change in the dad is the hair, I guess. He wears it close-cropped now that it's thinning and grey around the edges, but it suits him.

The littlest girl is taller, less chubby, and lets her hair flow long and straight, like her sister and mum's in the photo.

The big sister is taller too, much more beautiful,

a lot less adoring of the dad. Her hair is cut short at the back, long at the sides; an angular bob as sharp as her tongue.

The mum is gone, long gone, of course. About six months after the photo was taken, she was taken too, by the cancer no one knew was there.

Is it just coincidence that she's standing slightly apart from us in our joint pose? I don't know whether I'm happier thinking it was just coincidence or a premonition of things to come. . .

"Mum would've liked it here," Dad says softly, his deep voice vibrating the top of my head.

"Yep," I answer, nodding against his chest and hearing his heart boom-boom.

Mum hadn't really liked the Park Close house at first, Dad told us; one of his many Stories About Your Mum. But they were newly married at the time, expecting Clem, and it was all they could afford. She'd hoped they'd move on to some place old and full of character down the line. But then little Clem made friends, time passed, *I* came along and the next move never quite happened.

Well, not for Mum, at least.

"Hey, am I going to have to do *all* the work round here?" comes a grumble, as a girl-shaped black cloud stands silhouetted on the front doorstep.

She's only carrying a stool and her make-up box, but I guess it's better than nothing.

"Dad stuck the photo up," I tell her, untangling my arms from around Dad's waist and pointing into the kitchen.

Thankfully, Clem gives the stream of sarcasm a rest for a second and walks over to join us, to gaze at our once-upon-a-family.

"Hmm," she mumbles after a reflective second or two. "Bet she'd have hated it here."

With that, my sister thuds up the stairs, and Dad and I share conspiratorial grins, knowing Clem's oh-so-wrong. The mum Dad's described to us would've been looking in every cupboard, stroking the mantelpieces of the original fireplaces, planning to paint the neglected Victorian summerhouse in the overgrown garden.

"Well, better get this done!" Dad says brightly, bounding back out of the house, his good mood not in the least bit dented by Clem's gloom-fest.

That's my cue to get moving too, and I take the stairs two at a time, even though my box is heavy 'cause of the books inside.

"This place is such a dump," moans Clem, as I

reach the top landing and try to hurry past the door to my sister's new room. Her back is to me, but I know she likes an audience.

"It's not so bad," I try to placate her. "Not with your furniture in."

The general house stuff (beds, drawers, sofa, fridge, etc.); all of that got delivered an hour or so ago by a removal company, leaving the three of us behind at Park Close to pack the smaller stuff in the hire van, clean up, and say our goodbyes.

"Yeah, right!" says Clem, scuffing a toe at the threadbare patterned carpet. "It's a proper palace!"

I try to move on to *my* room, but she's got me trapped in her moaning force field.

"*And* it smells!"

"The air's just a bit stale," I say, my shoulders sagging with the weight of the box and Clem's negativity. "Every house or flat smells like this when no one's lived in it for a while."

The previous site manager had worked at Nightingale School and lived here for something crazy like thirty or forty years, Dad said.

He left about six months ago, and the school hadn't found the right candidate to fill his shoes, not till Dad came along.

"They smell like this when someone's *died* in them, Maisie!" says Clem, as if I am unspeakably naïve.

But no one *did* die here, did they? Dad made out that the old site manager just retired. Was that true? Or had Dad fluffed a white lie to keep me from stressing about the place?

"Did you hear what I said?" Clem calls out as I move away along the corridor.

"Nobody died, Clem," I reply flatly, hoping she doesn't hear the edge of uncertainty in my voice, or she'll think she's scored a point with me.

Instead I clatter into my room and kick the door closed with my heel.

Dropping the box and myself on the bed, I take a few deep, hopefully calming breaths.

I went through a phase when I was little, muddling fast-asleep dreams of Mum with half-awake sightings of her. Of course I know the difference now. I know there's no such thing as ghosts. But the very idea of them can make my grown-up, sensible heart race, just as madly as it did when the four-year-old me clung tight as a baby sloth to Dad during all those middle-of-the-night terrors.

What I need right now is the calm, reassuring

voice of a mother to tell me it'll be OK. That moving here was the right thing to do. That Dad made the best choice for us.

Luckily, I can make it happen – sort of.

Scrabbling open the cardboard flaps of the box, I reach in and pull out the faded, well-thumbed notebook.

The hard-backed cover is of a blue sky, a rainbow arching across it, a green meadow splatted with flowers.

Flip it open and the title page reads:

From Me To You

Thoughts from your mum,

for my darling girls. . .

Mum's notebook wasn't a secret; she'd pat her bed and me and Clem would clamber on, squishing right up to her, as she told us the latest words of wisdom she'd written down for us.

"This is for the two of you to look at together over the years, to share," she'd said with a smile, looking just a bit tired and not horribly ill, though that's what she was. "Promise?"

"Promise!" me and Clem had trilled together, linking pinkies with Mum, linking pinkies with each other, a little circle of love and trust.

My beloved Clem had smiled at me, a wide gap in the middle of her mouth where her two baby front teeth were missing. My heart went ping, knowing I was lucky enough to have the best big sister anyone could have: one who played tickle fights, pretended to be dogs with me, sang me silly songs in bed, held my hand tight, *tight* as we crossed roads, covered me with enthusiastic kisses.

But what a difference a decade makes.

Eighteen-year-old Clem spends most of her time being cross with me now. If I stay in the shower a minute too long, she's barking at me. If I drink the last of the orange juice in the fridge, she's ready to tear me apart.

And she'd absolutely freak out if she knew I'd written in the back of Mum's notebook, even though she never looks in it, ever.

She'd have a point. I shouldn't have done it – it's just that I'd really wanted Mum to "know" how I felt leaving our family home, of losing the view of the blue of the sky out of my bedroom window, of missing the flowery wallpaper Mum had chosen for me, of letting go of the feeling that she was somehow still in the walls. . .

My fingers have found the page I was looking for, and before I read the words, I glance up to see how blue the sky looks out of my *new* bedroom window.

Hmm . . . I can't see that much of it; the view of Nightingale School is in the way.

All I can make out are clouds scudding over the top of the building, which towers three storeys high – four, if you count the tiny windows of the turrets at either end.

I let my gaze drop slightly and lazily notice that above the grand front entrance with its double doors is a sort of terrace, though it must just be ornamental; the low brickwork along the edge is pretty (in a gothic way) rather than practical.

Then again, the three windows overlooking the terrace are extra long, as if you could step out there and escape the classroom if you felt like it.

Wonder which classroom that is? Will it be one I use when I start school on Monday?

My tummy twists itself into a squidgy knot of excitement and nerves at the very thought. What will the other girls be like, I won—

That thought stops dead.

The knot suddenly tightens, like iron.

It's Saturday.

The school is all locked up and empty.

But there is someone standing in the left-hand window of the three overlooking the terrace.

The person is dressed in white.

Their hand is on the glass.

They are looking straight at me. . .

Always listen to your dad – he has your best interests at heart.

"But what was it?" I say, staring at the big, blank window to the left, directly above the terrace.

We've been staring at it for ages now – there's no one and nothing there.

"Sunlight hitting the window . . . or maybe the reflection of a cloud, or a plane?" Dad suggests.

"Maybe," I agree, feeling calm and common sense creeping over me, banishing the freak-out.

"Or maybe not," says Clem from the doorway. "It's probably the ghost of the old guy who lived here, wandering the corridors."

"Clem, honey – that's not helping!" Dad chides her gently.

"Hey, it's not MY fault we've come to live in some haunted dump," she grumbles, turning away and disappearing into her room with a thwack of the door.

"She'll get used it," Dad says to me with a hopeful smile.

Or we'll just have to get used to her moaning about this place 24-7, I think to myself.

"So, are we all good?" Dad asks, jokily bumping me with his elbow.

"We're all good," I say with a grin, bumping him right back.

I'm always all good with whatever Dad says and does. It's like Mum wrote in her notebook (which I picked up off the floor and tucked under my pillow): he's worth listening to, 'cause he always has our best interests at heart. So if Dad says there're no spooks lurking in Nightingale School, then there're no spooks lurking in Nightingale School.

Anyway, I know for sure it wasn't some old bloke ghost like Clem is trying to get me to believe.

That trick of the light or reflection of a cloud or a plane or whatever; it looked more like a woman. Or a girl. . .

"Fancy an explore, then?"

Dad suddenly holds up a bunch of keys so huge it's a joke. There must be forty, fifty of them.

"Come on . . . let's do it!" he says with a wide grin.

I'm up for it.

Clem isn't.

"Uh-uh. I'm staying here," she says, arms folded across her chest, when Dad tries to entice her out of her room.

"Come on, my little Clementine. Don't you want to investigate your new home?" Dad asks her, jangling the keys in front of her face.

"Dad, out there is the *school.* That is not my home. *This* dump is my new home. I know it has three bedrooms, a bathroom from the Dark Ages, a weird smell – 'cause some old person *died* in here – and generally sucks. That's as much as I need to know."

"Honey, no one died here," says Dad, sounding like me earlier. "Anyway, aren't you the tiniest bit curious to know more about the school and the grounds?"

"Not even *that* much," Clem replies, squidging her finger and thumb tightly together.

"But what about when Bea and your other friends ask you about the place?"

"Dad, no one except you – and Maisie – are *remotely* interested in the fact that we've moved here."

I'm not totally sure about that. I have a memory of Clem's mates Bea, Marcus and Alima huddled round the computer, checking out the street view of the cottage on Google Maps. Dad was pointing out the front garden and front door through the railings, and telling them that as well as a back garden and back door, we *also* had a side door that opened out directly on to the playground. The whole time, Clem had stood apart, clutching her mug of coffee so her knuckles went white, quietly seething at her friends' enthusiasm.

"Well, I'm not taking no for an answer," Dad says cheerily now, steamrollering over my sister's flat refusals. "Come on my guided tour just this once, Clem, and I promise you I'll never expect you to step a toe on to school property again!"

Clem sighs.

Clem rolls her eyes.

Clem mutters something under her breath that I suspect might be a swear word.

Dad pulls a puppy-dog face at her, his hands up in begging mode.

It works; Clem gives in and grudgingly follows us out of the side door for a mooch around the grounds.

"It's beautiful!" I gasp, gazing at the vast lawn of the bottom playground. I'd peeked at it out of Dad's bedroom, noticed it beyond our tangled back garden and tatty, pointy-roofed summerhouse. But close up it's so lovely, the sheet of green dotted with pink-petalled bundles dropped from the cherry blossom trees.

"It's going to take a lot of cutting," says Dad, eyeing up the sea of grass where girls like me must spend their lunchtimes lounging.

(The thought of starting school on Monday makes that knot in my tummy go *squidge* all over again.)

Clem keeps her eyes firmly averted from the view, her fingers flying over her mobile as she texts her grievances to Bea or one of the others.

She's barely aware of us moving on.

"It looks new!" I say in surprise as we wander into the top playground and see a purpose-built multi-sports court.

"Just because Nightingale School is a-hundred-and-something years old, it doesn't mean the place is full of out-of-date equipment!" Dad laughs. "Wait till you see the ICT Suite. . ."

The school I used to go to was only as old as the housing estate we lived on. The classrooms were big and bright; the playground was small and crowded.

Nightingale is like a different world.

"Welcome to your new home-from-home," Dad says, leading the way over to a dark blue door at the side of the building, jangling his keys at me.

"It's not MY home-from-home," mumbles Clem, diverting away from us, arms crossed, heading back towards the cottage. "Have fun!"

With a sarky wiggle of her fingers, she's gone.

Which is a relief, actually. When she's in one of her moods (which is most of the time), having Clem around can be as much fun as swimming in cement.

Stepping alone into the cool cream corridor with Dad, I'm instantly lighter, allowed to be excited without my sister's scorn spoiling things.

Straightaway, Dad has something to show me.

"Here's my office," he says, unlocking a door that leads to a small, functional room.

"Great!" I say, though there's not much to see. "So, do I have to call you *this* now?"

I'm smiling as I point at a sign on the door he's relocking. It reads *Site Manager* in a large, bold font, with *Mr J. Butterfield* underneath it.

Butterfield.

I like that name. It sounds nicely old-fashioned or slightly funny or even vaguely familiar, somehow.

"My predecessor," says Dad, talking, of course, about the previous owner of our cottage. "I'll ask the ladies in the school office to have it updated on Monday."

I wish that tummy knot would stop squidging whenever I'm reminded of my looming first morning at school. I just want to enjoy the newness of all this, not feel flurries of fear.

I think Dad spots the muddle I'm in.

"Hey, you can be who you want to be here, honey," Dad says, giving my shoulders a squeeze. "You can reinvent yourself, or just get back to being the *old* Maisie Mills!"

The old Maisie Mills . . . *that* sounds good. Till a couple of terms ago, the old Maisie Mills was all anyone knew at school.

The old Maisie Mills was carefree and fun, someone pretty well-liked by everyone, especially the teachers, especially her for ever best friends, Lilah and Jasneet. The old Maisie Mills smiled a lot, chatted a lot, laughed a lot.

And then everything changed.

The new Maisie Mills was hurt and angry most of the time, unless she was safe at home with Dad. The new Maisie Mills confused people – especially the teachers – by crying in class, in the playground, in the loos. The new Maisie Mills was mostly silent, since no one believed her any more. The new Maisie Mills had nothing to smile or laugh about. . .

I give myself a sudden shake – I'm getting all pretentious and dramatic again.

"You can properly close the door on all of the stuff that went on, honey," Dad says, reading my mind again, as we begin to open door after door to classrooms covered in projects made by girls I don't know yet, girls who might be my new best friends, better than the old best friends by a mile.

"I love it! I love it all!" I tell Dad, as we head up the grand, sweeping staircase, with its Art Nouveau flowered wall tiles and a thick wooden banister that's worn to a deep, dull shine with more than a century's worth of girls' hands gliding up and down it.

"And you haven't seen the best bit yet," says Dad, beaming at me, happy to see *me* so happy.

We're on the first floor, outside a door that's got the most beautiful patterned frosted-glass panel. The white swirls and leaves are echoed in the windows that stretch along the corridor, screening whatever's inside.

"What's this, then?" I ask, as Dad turns a key

in a chunky brass lock and grasps the matching doorknob.

"The art room," he replies. "But the word 'room' doesn't really do it justice!"

He's right – we step into a huge space, almost the size of the gym at my old school. It's like being in a gallery: paintings, drawings, collages cover every inch of wall, jostling for my attention. Pots, sculptures, modelling projects teeter on tables and cupboard surfaces. Some kind of suspended junk sculpture – maybe you'd call it an installation? – made out of old drinks bottles and CDs twirls gently from the hook and rope it's dangling from.

"Brilliant, isn't it?" Dad says, sounding as if he's an estate agent proudly showing off his prize property.

"Uh-huh," I murmur, trying to take it all in. It's about a million times better than the art rooms in my old school. My teacher, Miss Stephens, would just flip through a few images of Mondrian or whoever and tells us to copy the style. Here, it looks like a wonderland of possibilities.

Please let that go for *everything* about this school. . .

"Hey, you know something, Maisie? I'll bet *this* is what you saw from your bedroom window!" says

Dad, pointing to the junk sculpture.

Of course.

Of course we're in the room with the three long windows. I hurry over to look out of one of them – the one I thought I saw the face in – and gaze across the roof terrace just outside, across the playground to our cottage. My bedroom window is like an eye peeking up at me (the other "eye" belongs to Clem's room; I can see her now, angrily trying to put up curtains).

"Of course," I say out loud, turning and letting my fingers linger over the plastic bottles and shiny CDs that I'd mistaken for a ghost.

"Oops – better get back," says Dad, checking his watch. "I need to get the computer set up so we can make contact with the outside world!"

I smile a secret smile as I go to follow him out.

By outside world, I know he's really talking about Donna. They email and Facebook each other every day, and she'll be dying to hear how the move went.

Hey, maybe Dad will invite Donna to come see the place? And give me and Clem the chance to finally meet her? Surely after all these months of dating, Dad can relax enough to introduce us to each other? It's not as if either me or Clem will give her a hard time. We both know Mum's thoughts on Dad having a "new relationship", thanks to what she wrote in the notebo—

The rustle and clunk makes me spin around, just as I reach the open doorway.

It's the plastic bottle and CD installation, dancing around like it's doing the salsa in some sudden breeze that's blown in.

"Dad, I think one of the windows must be open," I tell him.

Then a chill settles over me, as I spot all of the windows firmly shut and locked.

"Hmm?" says Dad distractedly, checking his phone for Donna-texts.

"Nothing," I mutter, desperate to get outside to the air and the sunshine of the playground. . .

3

Look out for each other,

all three of you.

"What? Seen your ghost again?" asks Clem, wandering into the bathroom and frowning at me.

She's not looking like my super-sleek sis right now; she's in her first-thing-in-the-morning disguise of Fuzzy Grouch Monster. She might be addicted to high-street fashion and hair straighteners for vast chunks of the day, but pre-breakfast she's this sour-faced blur with hair like knitting gone wrong and a dressing gown that's so faded it's hard to guess what colour the dots on it started out as (it used to be Mum's).

"What?" I ask, blinking at her as I come out of my fug of panicky thoughts.

There is no ghost. There's only some dumb art project that I must have brushed by on Saturday as I went to follow Dad out of the art room. And when I brushed past it, it rattled, which rattled *me*.

What's really real, though, is that it's Monday, it's 8.25 a.m., and – unlike my sister with her almost part-time sixth-form timetable – I have to be in school in five minutes. My new school. With new people. Who I don't know and who don't know me. I won't know where my classrooms are and I won't know who to ask to show me.

"I'm talking about your *face*, Maisie – it's as if you've seen a ghost. It's like this!" Clem says, then does something with her own face that makes it look like a zombie who's just seen a horror movie.

"No, it's not!" I snap back, then get up from my perch on the edge of the bath where I've been sitting as I brush my teeth.

Gazing at myself in the mirror above the sink, I realize I *do* look pale, as if my skin hasn't seen sunshine for a very long time, or like a vampire sucked my blood in the night. And I guess there is a hint of complete and total panic about my eyes.

"Look, I know you're nervous about today, Maisie, and yeah, it'll be weird for the first hour or whatever," says Clem, twisting the shower knob on. "But you've just got to get on with it and get over yourself."

So *that's* Clem's kind, thoughtful advice as I head out to my first day at Nightingale School? Gee, thanks.

It makes me think of one of Mum's notebook instructions: *Look out for each other, all three of you.*

I mean, if telling me to get over myself is an example of Clem looking out for me, then I'm doomed. . .

"Well?"

"Well, what?" I say, turning away from the mirror image of the scared girl in her new school uniform.

"Well, can I have some space, please?" says Clem, shooing me out of the bathroom.

I turn to go, and only realize I'm still holding my toothbrush once the door slams shut behind me and the bolt clunks to lock it.

It's all right for Clem, I grump to myself as I pad downstairs. She has most of the same friends now in sixth form as she had in nursery. She's never had to change schools. She's never had the experience of being shunned by her best mates, and treated like she's a little bit worse than toxic by everyone in her class. . .

I grab my bag, take a deep breath and get ready

for my walk to school, which will take all my tattered courage and exactly seventy-six steps door to door (I did a trial run yesterday, in the still of Sunday morning).

Here we go. . . I open the side door that leads directly into the packed playground, where I see girls streaming through the big main gates, laughing, chatting, arms linked. There are so, so many of them, but I guess it's the same as my last school: eight form classes in each year group.

Maybe it's just an optical illusion; the playground seems packed because there're no boys to break up the sea of navy-dressed girls.

Will it be strange being at a school with no boys, I wonder?

The positive side to it is the maths: eight classes times thirty-girls-to-a-class equals two hundred and forty students in my year. Out of those two hundred and forty, surely I'll find *one* friend at least?

But right this second it's hard to be positive and think of potential friend equations, 'cause my first-day panic is rising like the temperature in a toaster and I feel like something inside is about to pop.

"Walk," I whisper an order to myself.

Five steps: my heart is beating so frantically it's as

if there's a ticking time bomb in my ribcage.

Ten steps: I try to remind myself how I felt on Saturday morning when we unlocked the creaking front door to our new home. The giddy feeling of freedom from my old life, thanks to this shiny new start. . .

Fifteen steps: I give up on recapturing the giddy feeling and just try not to throw up with nerves.

"Hey, you're looking great!" Dad calls out to me, making a few nearby girls turn their heads to see who the new site manager is talking to. I can tell from their gazes that they don't share his opinion. A pale-faced, scared girl in a slightly-too-big blazer does not look great. Except to her dad, I guess.

"Don't know about that," I reply, trying to conjure up a half-convincing smile for him.

"So, are we all good?" he asks, his blue eyes staring into my brown ones, willing me to be OK.

I look at him in his khaki workshirt and jeans, a stray traffic cone under his arm, left over from the line he's just set up outside the school gates to dissuade cars from dropping off students where they shouldn't.

If I wasn't feeling sick, I'd probably make a joke about the traffic cone being his new hat, and if he wasn't busy on his first day, he'd probably put it on, at a jaunty angle.

"Mm-hm," I mumble, not able to answer him in a whole sentence, since my fake smile is about to go wobbly. And even if I'm *normally* good with what Dad says, there's always an exception to a rule, isn't there?

"It won't be as bad as you think, Maisie. I bet you'll come out buzzing at the end of the day, and have a bunch of new friends straightaway!"

"Mm-hm," I mumble again, then turn to go, aiming myself towards the stern double doors of the main entrance, feeling less like plain Maisie Mills and more like I'm Mary, Queen of Scots, heading for the looming executioner and the chopping block.

Though I'm actually heading for the school office, which I know – thanks to Saturday's guided tour of the empty building – is just inside the open doors, to the right.

"Yes?" says a white-haired woman on the other side of the varnished dark wood counter.

It's the sort of moment where you don't know whether your voice will work and whether you'll remember your own name.

"Um, hello," I thankfully manage to squeak. "I'm Maisie Mills. I'm starting today in Year Eight."

"Ah, Maisie Mills. . . Maisie Mills. . ." the woman says, an edge of something uncertain in her voice. "Can you hold on just a second?"

She trots off in her clicky-clacky kitten-heel shoes and talks to a larger woman at a desk, whose dark, braided hair has hints of grey woven in it. The two ladies have some sort of animated but very hushed conversation which involves sideways glances at me. In other words, they are in a total flap 'cause I've turned up. This is making me feel less than fantastic.

"Sorry, my love," says the bigger lady of the two – the one with the braided hair – while handing me a map of the school and a timetable. "We *have* been expecting you, but there's been a slight problem. Still, nothing for you to worry about; just follow me!"

And so I follow, up stairs, down corridors, listening to what the woman is saying, while wishing I was like Hansel and Gretel and had white pebbles to leave behind me as a trail, so I can find my way out of this school maze later.

What the braided-haired lady has been telling me includes this. . . Her name is Mahalia, and the other lady in the office is June, and I have to come see them if I have any problems.

My new form tutor is called Mrs Watson.

She has done a detailed transition plan for me.

Mrs Watson is off sick today.

No one can find the detailed transition plan.

Turns out, *that's* my main problem today, and it doesn't seem like either Mahalia or June can help with it. . .

"So here we are, my love!" says Mahalia, standing in front of a door and rapping on it.

She opens it before the teacher inside has even said "Come in!", so my first class of the day, the week, the rest of my school life kicks off with a teacher glowering at me.

And don't even *mention* the twenty-nine girls' faces staring blankly.

Excuse me while I run away. . .

You know what?

What Dad said first thing today, about school not being so bad, how I'd come out buzzing, how I'd make a bunch of friends straightaway?

Well, it was.

I didn't.

I double didn't.

"You said it yourself, Maisie: if your form teacher hadn't been off ill today, it would've been OK," says Dad, putting down his fork and patting my hand.

The patting doesn't do much to reassure me. I feel like there's a heavy black fog in my head, trying to block out the sharp, uncomfortable flashbacks I'm having of the day. Right now I'm picturing the glowering maths teacher, who did at least stop glowering once she realized Mahalia had interrupted her lesson for a good reason (if you can call *me* a good reason).

But she seemed as flustered as the office ladies had been when I first turned up. She pointed at a spare seat, and got someone to pass me back a workbook to write in. I sat for the entire lesson hearing nothing, understanding nothing in my panic.

It got much better after that – *not*.

Seems that the teachers at Nightingale are super-strict about filing in and out of class silently, so no one talked to me at the end of that first lesson. Though why would they even have wanted to? I'd been so excited at the idea of starting over, but until I was sitting there in that first class, it hadn't occurred to me that all the girls would probably be tight friends anyway – the last thing they'd want was some newbie like me trying to muscle my way into their cliques.

So when the end-of-lesson bell went, I pretended to rummage in my bag for something. A couple of girls stared back over their shoulders, but I hovered some more, letting everyone drift away to their next classes, while I figured my own way using the timetable and map.

And that was the pattern of the day. Being last one into class; being last one out; keeping my head down and wandering round clutching my crumpled map.

Of course, that pattern was broken up nicely with break time (spent it in a cubicle in the girls' loos) and lunchtime (couldn't face it and snuck home).

As first days go, it could only have got worse if a stray asteroid had crashed into the school.

Mind you, that might have been a blessing in disguise and put me out of my misery. . .

"Hi, I'm home – if you can call it that!" Clem calls out, barging in with a slam of the front door and a thud of her bag full of textbooks.

"Hi, honey! Thought you were coming home for

tea?" Dad shouts back in a friendly-but-making-a-point way.

"Fancied hanging out at Bea's," Clem replies casually, plonking down on to a chair and plucking a meatball out of the spaghetti on Dad's plate.

"Yours is in the microwave," says Dad. "And didn't you have your phone on you?"

"Huh?" Clem answers, and we realize she still has her earphones in and can only semi-hear what Dad's saying.

"Never mind," he says, giving up before there's a fight and an atmosphere. Or maybe it's because he's got me and my blue mood to deal with and can't be doing with a Clem huff on top of it.

"Uh-oh. You've got your zombie face on again, Maisie!" says my sister, suddenly staring straight at me. "Bad day at Planet School, then?"

"Pretty much," I reply, using my fork to swirl my spaghetti into uneaten spirals on my plate.

"Yeah, so? What happened?" she asks, in a distracted way that makes me feel like my lousy day will either amuse or bore her.

"It just wasn't great," I say, not wanting to see her roll her eyes at my woes. "Going to the loo – back in a minute."

The loo thing is an excuse to get away from Clem's half-hearted interrogation, Dad's hangdog expression of disappointment, and the pile of food I'm not going to eat.

Instead I go into my room, still stacked with boxes yet to be unpacked, and rest my forehead on the cool of the windowpane.

Urgh, I feel so achingly *sad*. . .

Not just because my first day was confusing and worrying.

But also because it's dawned on me today that despite Mum's scribbled hope, I can't rely on Clem to look out for me *ever*, and despite his best intentions, Dad just isn't able to look out for me all the time either.

I mean, he couldn't do it when all that stuff happened with Saffy and Lilah and Jasneet, could he? No matter what Dad said, my head teacher believed *them*, not me; three against one.

And he couldn't say or do anything to make today all right, same as he can't make tomorrow any better.

Just how am I going to get through thi—

Suddenly I freeze, seized with shock.

It's there again. . .

The figure at the art room window!

I lean on the ledge, squinting hard, trying to see how that human-looking shape could be the dangling pile of plastic bottles and CDs.

It could be, I suppose.

Only I can't see how it would have a *face*.

As my heart races, a thought occurs to me.

There's something I could try, just to be sure. Sure of something I don't understand.

I lift my hand up and wave. . .

And the figure in the window waves back.

4

Be confident in yourself – even if you feel shy and nervous.

Another morning.

My second day at Nightingale School.

"I am SO sorry about yesterday, Maisie!" says Mrs Watson, who is placing a small plate of chocolate biscuits in front of me. She waves her hand towards them, so I know I'm allowed to help myself, that it's not just some teacher's treat.

We're sitting in her bright, neat office, which has a view of the back playground and the multi-sports court.

I knew to come here today 'cause Dad texted me from his standpoint by the traffic cones earlier, telling me Mrs Watson had hurriedly introduced herself to him and told him that she wanted me to report to her first thing.

I'd panicked a bit about that; *how* was I meant to

report to her? Where would I find her?

But there in the reception area was a woman with neat, short hair and a matching neat skirt suit reaching a hand out to shake my trembling one and barking, "You must be Maisie; I've been on the lookout for you!" in a loud but kindly voice.

She's apologized for being off ill about twelve times already, but you know, I like this chocolate-biscuit-flavoured apology best.

And I like *her*.

The more Mrs Watson talks, the more I feel the tightly wound springs inside me begin to uncoil and release. Suddenly, I feel hungry. Which is no surprise, since all I did was swirl my tea last night and eat about two teaspoonfuls of Cheerios this morning.

I take a biscuit in the shape of a small doughnut and eat it in one go.

"Anyway, I know it's not easy coming into a year group halfway through a term, Maisie," Mrs Watson breezes on. "But I'm sure you'll come to love everything about Nightingale School."

What – even its ghost? I think, as I try to crunch quietly and politely.

Immediately, I give a little twitch, trying to shake that stupid thought away.

Yes, there was someone in the art room about six-ish last night. But it was probably the teacher, hanging back to mark work or plan the next day's lesson. Or it was a cleaner, maybe.

I didn't say anything to Dad this time; he looked at me like a kicked puppy when I finally came downstairs yesterday. This job is too important – it's *everything* – to go worrying him about things I *imagined* I was seeing.

(I don't want to think about the fact that the teacher or cleaner or whoever at the window looked a lot like the figure I saw on Saturday morning. The one that was just a trick of the light; a reflection; the twirling junk sculpture, maybe. . .)

"And I'm guessing you might be a bit concerned about all the existing friendship groups in class. Well, the girls here really are very nice, so if you can just try to have confidence in yourself and give it time, you'll settle in, I'm sure!"

I choke slightly at the word *confidence*. Last night I flicked through Mum's notebook and found myself staring at the page that read: *Be confident in yourself* –

even if you feel shy and nervous.

"All right?" says Mrs Watson, reaching over and giving me a friendly thump on the back.

I really hope so, I say silently to myself, crossing my chocolatey fingers as I struggle for breath. . .

I'm eating my lunch *very* slowly.

Not because I'm stressed about choking, but because lots of people are hunched around, lobbing questions at me like tennis balls.

It's a change from the loneliness of yesterday, that's for sure, and it's all thanks to Mrs Watson. She's assigned two different girls to be my "minders" every day this week, to help me find my way around *and* help me get to know people, I guess.

Today it's the turn of Hannah and Patience.

Up till now they've marched me between classes like efficient nurses, talking at me, telling me where things are, what the teachers are like. Neither of them has asked me much about myself so far, but all the girls huddled round are more than making up for it now.

"What was the name of your old school?"

"Park View."

"Yeah? Don't know it. Do you, Bella?"

"No. Was it OK there?"

"Yeah, it was all right."

"Were there boys at Park View school, or was it just girls, like here?"

"Uh, there were boys too."

"What was *that* like?"

"It was mostly all right," I say with a shrug, answering the mass of faces staring at me. Well, about eight or nine faces, I reckon, but that's enough to fluster me, even though I really *want* the company.

"So, is it true that your dad's, like, the *caretaker* here?" says a girl who I think is called Libby or Livvy, maybe.

(I'm sure I hear someone on the outer edge of the gaggle of girls giggle, and mutter something about "emptying bins". But maybe I'm just being paranoid.)

"*Site manager*, Libby!" another girl corrects her, who I remember for sure is Natasha. "The only place Mr Mills would be called a 'caretaker' is if he was in an episode of *Scooby Doo*, being unmasked as the bad guy! He's not a bad guy, is he, Maisie?"

"Er, no. . ."

Uh-oh. Is this Natasha taking the mickey out of my dad too, only in a more subtle way?

"So is that what he's always done, been the site manager at different schools?" asks someone called Rose or Rosie.

"No – this is the first time."

"What did he do before?" That's Hannah.

"He worked for a consultancy, but he got made redundant."

At the words "consultancy", I can see my classmates' eyes glazing over.

"So, what's it like living *right* in the school, practically?" asks Bella, steering away from that boring topic.

"Um. . ." I say, thinking about how I feel. "I'm not sure yet."

"Your dad seems nice," Libby adds. "At least he's a lot younger than Mr Butterfield. He was so ancient we used to worry he'd keel over one day in the playground!"

"Did he? Die, I mean?" I ask, spotting a chance to find out more about our home's former owner.

"No!" snorts Libby. "He just retired. The head presented him with this *boooring* clock at assembly one day, remember?"

She turns to look at the others, who all nod and remember too.

I allow myself to smile inside, looking forward to blowing Clem's theory about Mr Butterfield dying in the house.

Then I jump when I realize Hannah has said something to me.

"What's so funny?"

Oh . . . was I smiling on the outside too?

"Um, nothing," I mumble, feeling instantly tense.

"Were you really sad to leave your old friends?" Patience asks, and I find myself wondering if she senses my anxiety, and has helped me out by flinging another question my way. Pity it's one that's difficult to answer truthfully, and not get into a long story I'd rather avoid.

So I go for a white lie.

"A bit."

"Bet you were all crying on your last day!" Patience adds.

"Mmm."

My answers aren't too interesting, I guess. There's an awkward few moments, where the questions peter out, the girls' interest in me seeming to stutter and falter – even Patience loses her patience, and glances sideways at the others.

The silence probably lasts all of two or three seconds, but it's long enough for me to feel the wave of panic roll in. I spent a horrible chunk of time at my last school with no one talking much to me, and the thought of that happening again makes me feel scared and hopeless.

Sorry, Mum; I know you wrote what you wrote in your notebook 'cause you hoped it would help, but I can't rely on confidence to get me through this. Any slivers of self-confidence I might have had once upon a time got mashed up and mushed up quite a while back.

But I *can* try something else.

Take a breath, Maisie.

Don't think about it.

Just say it – and *quickly*.

"Can I tell you something that might sound weird?" I start, heart thudding at the risk I'm taking. These girls might think I'm completely insane. . .

"Go on!" says Patience, her dark eyes widening with interest.

OK. Here goes.

"A couple of times from my bedroom window . . .

I've thought I've seen something in the art room window. Some*one*, I mean. But at times when there shouldn't be anyone in school."

There's a micro-second's quiet where I hold my breath, wondering how they're going to respond.

And then Patience gives an excited squeal, while Hannah shrieks at a couple of people on the next table.

"She's seen it! Maisie the new girl has seen the ghost!!"

Whooaa . . . what a relief. They *don't* think I'm crazy. I've done it; I said something that made them take notice of me again.

"What did she look like?"

"Was she in this long, sweeping Victorian dress?"

"Was she scary?"

"Or sad?"

"Were you frightened?"

"Was she about our age?"

"Was she pretty?

"Or like a skeleton or something!"

"Did she seem like she had a broken neck?"

With the jabber of voices all talking at once, I don't know who to answer first, so I try a question myself.

"So there *is* a ghost?" I ask incredulously, tiny shivers rippling up and down my back.

"Oh, *absolutely*!" says Natasha, taking control of the conversation as more girls crowd eagerly around us. "But come on; what did she look like to you?"

"Just a girl, or young woman, dressed in white," I tell my excited audience. "Which of *you* have seen it?"

"Oh, none of *us* have ever seen it," says Natasha.

My excitement dips slightly, as the assembled girls shake their heads in disappointed agreement.

"But plenty of people have in the past, or we wouldn't know about it, would we?!" says Natasha, undeterred.

"Yeah, Ella in 8H, her auntie saw it when *she* was at school here years ago," Hannah butts in.

"And that Marta girl in Year Eleven; her big cousin saw it too, when she first started at Nightingale," adds Patience.

"Anyway," Natasha carries on, "it's supposed to be the ghost of this girl who went to school here when it was first built back in eighteen . . . eighteen-something-or-other, and she roams the corridors –"

"Woo-OOOOOO-ooooo!" Rose (or Rosie) joins

in, with fitting sound effects and wafty hands.

"– trying to solve the mystery of what happened to her!"

"And what *did* happen to her?" I ask, gripped by this new twist in my very own tale. My mouth feels dry, even though the glass of water beside me is nearly empty.

"She had a terrible accident, and her neck was broken, like this," says Natasha, miming a very dead person, tongue lolling.

"Ah, but *was* it an accident?" Libby jumps in. "'Cause maybe—"

"Maybe you ladies need to get to your first afternoon class!" a voice interrupts.

Mrs Watson, standing unnoticed just behind some of the gathered girls, has a grin of amusement on her face, even if she's trying to be stern.

"But Mrs Watson, we were just telling Maisie about—"

"I *heard* what you and Libby were telling Maisie about, Natasha, and you *know* that it's just a silly story. So chop, chop . . . let's move it out and beat the bell!"

As Mrs Watson marches off, she gives me a wink over her shoulder. Luckily, it doesn't seem as if she heard *my* part of the conversation or she might be dragging me to one side to tell me off for spoofing the other girls.

But there's no time to think about Victorian ghosts right now, even though that's exactly what I want to do, of course. The end-of-lunch bell shrills deafeningly, so I copy everyone around me and screech back my chair, hauling my school bag up on my back.

I go to follow Hannah and Patience, who are up ahead of me, chatting excitedly together, when a hand on my shoulder stops me where I am.

Turning, I see a girl I'd vaguely spotted hovering at the edge of the circle of girls who'd gathered around me. She's smiling shyly, like she wants to say something to me.

"Hi – I'm Kat. Kat with a 'K'," she says.

Kat with a 'K' is pretty, with all this tousled, fair hair just past her shoulders, held back with a silky navy scarf, tied in a cute, fat, slouchy bow at the top of her head. But she is wearing a bit too much make-up – her lashes are thick with mascara and her cheeks are pinked up with very obvious rosy-brown blusher. Won't she get into trouble for that?

"I'm Maisie," I say stupidly, since she'll know that already if she's in my class. Then again, maybe she's not, since I haven't managed to imprint everyone's faces in my head yet.

"I'm not in your form class," the girl answers my silent fret. "But I just wanted to come over and say. . ."

Kat with a 'K' hesitates for a second, biting at her bottom lip, shiny with some shimmery sort of balm.

". . .well, you're not kidding, are you?" she finally whispers. "You really *did* see a ghost, didn't you?"

As Kat's inquisitive eyes twinkle hopefully, a thought occurs to me.

"Have you seen it too?" I whisper back.

"Nope," she says, linking her arm into mine as the crowds of girls surge us forward. "But I'd *love* to find out her story!"

As I feel the surprising closeness of her, *another* thought occurs to me.

Could Kat with a "K" become a friend, perhaps?

A friend I could go on a ghost-hunt with?

I feel like giving a little skip, but I don't want to frighten her off. . .

5

Please stay open-minded if Dad meets someone new.

It's Wednesday lunchtime, and it seems that ghosts are yesterday's news.

Today, the girls from my class are huddling around the long dining table, discussing just how revolting today's lunch is and whether or not it's true that some sixth former I don't know has been suspended for coming into school with a pierced lip this morning.

"Well, I guess it's better than having a piercing in your *tongue*!" says Libby, wincing.

"Or one of those auricle piercings – that's got to hurt!" says Natasha, pulling a face like she's sucked a lemon.

"What's an auricle?" I ask, then feel my face flush, in case it's somewhere rude.

All the girls stare at me, then burst out laughing.

"You thought it was somewhere rude, didn't you?" Hannah guesses.

Yes, OK, so they're right, but I can't stand being laughed at. I get that enough at home from Clem. And when they weren't ignoring me at my last school, there was plenty of sniggering going on behind my back too.

"I'm just going to tidy this away," I tell them, ready to take my tray – and my red face – to the far side of the dining hall.

"It's in the muscle of your ear, Maisie!" Patience calls out.

I keep walking, wishing she hadn't shouted that out. Now everyone will be swivelling their heads around to stare at me. That happened a lot at my old school too. . .

"Boo!"

Kat suddenly appears in front of me, her head tilted, her fat, slouchy bow flopping to one side of her head.

"Hello!" I say, perking up at the sight of her.

I've been keeping a lookout for her since yesterday morning, since our rushed conversation in the dining hall. No sooner had we linked arms than a crush of Year 7s had run past us, forcing us apart, and she headed off to her class with a wave and a smile over bobbing heads.

After school, I hovered in the playground, hoping to catch her, but hundreds of girls were pouring out of side doors, back doors, main doors, and she was lost amongst them.

I hovered again this morning, saying shy hellos to my new classmates as they wandered by, but again, I didn't see Kat in the crush of navy blazers.

And at lunchtime just now, I spent all my time gazing around for her, while the girls in my class chattered endlessly about the bogging bolognese and the dodgy lip piercing. (Seems they're already over the novelty of me, as well as the subject of ghosts.)

I'd just got up a second ago to tidy my tray away, and here, at last, is Kat, blocking my way with a smile and a boo.

"Want to come with me?" Kat asks, a mischievous little grin on her face.

"Um, OK," I reply, intrigued and excited.

Out of the corner of my eye I see Natasha and Libby – my minders for today – watch me wander away. From the blank expressions on their faces they don't seem exactly bothered about where I might be going. The girl with the lip piercing beats me hands down when it comes to their interest levels. Actually, the disgustingness of the bolognese probably beats me too, in their eyes.

"How's it going with that lot?" Kat asks, throwing her thumb over her shoulder at the crew from 8E.

"OK, I guess."

I give a non-committal shrug as I follow Kat out of the dining hall and across the playground, veering around gaggles of drifting, chatting girls.

"You don't *look* all that sure," says Kat, throwing me a wry smile.

"I guess it's just weird when you're new," I say, unsure how I feel about my classmates, how they feel about me, how honest to be with Kat, since we've only just met.

"Hey, it's weird when you've been here for ever too," she answers, her smile suddenly dipping behind a cloud of a frown.

Oh. That frown seems familiar – the last few months I saw that exact same expression whenever I caught sight of my reflection in the mirrors in the Park View girls' loos. Does Kat have friendship hassles too, I wonder?

It seems too rude, too soon to come right out and ask, so I say something more vague.

"So what's *your* form class like?"

"I don't really hang out with any of them," says Kat, stomping faster across the playground.

Wow, I was right! Something's happened, something broke . . . same as me and my old friends my old school. Wonder what it is? Whatever, maybe it's all meant to be. Maybe it's the reason we just clicked – that and the mystery of the face at the window. . .

"Where exactly did you see her?" says Kat, changing the subject, same as *I* used to do when Dad asked if everything was OK when it absolutely wasn't.

"The ghost, you mean?" I whisper at Kat's back, as I half-run to keep up with her.

"Well, yeah!" Kat turns and laughs at me over her shoulder. "Who else?"

I check that she's not laughing *at* me – like Clem does, like people at my old school did, like the girls in my form class did just now.

But her blue eyes are friendly and her smile is all warmth. And it's great to see the frown gone.

"It was that one," I tell her, pointing up to the terrace above the front door, to the long window on the left.

"I *thought* that's the one you meant – let's go!"

And so we go: scooting through the main doors of the building, zipping up the swooping staircase, and breathlessly finding ourselves at an open door that leads into the huge art room.

"What are we doing here?" I ask Kat nervously. The room is full of girls from all year groups, either bent over drawing or yakking with friends. Some kind of classical music drifts from a paint-splattered CD player in the corner, by a collection of half-decorated wonky pots.

"It's Art Club here on a Wednesday lunchtime. You just need to go and introduce yourself to the teacher."

Kat gives me a nudge, propelling me and my reluctant legs over towards a woman in jeans and a long once-white apron who's got one arm deep in a chipped old sink, awkwardly, single-handedly washing brushes.

"Um, hi – I'm Maisie, I'm new," I manage to say.

The teacher turns to me and smiles.

"Welcome to Art Club, Maisie-who's-new!" she jokes. "I'm Miss Carrera. As you'll see, we're very relaxed here."

I can tell they are. And I can see why a girl

who maybe doesn't fit in with her class might like hanging out in here.

"Just help yourself to paper, pencils, paint . . . or grab an art book and flick through it for inspiration," Miss Carrera carries on. "Or you could just sit around and daydream till inspiration comes to you!"

I nod apologetically and back away, 'cause I've just spotted that she's got a phone in her free hand, and that I've interrupted her conversation.

Quickly glancing around, I see Kat over at the window. I mean, THE window. I snake my way between the tables, past the swaying junk sculpture, the heady scent of paints and chalks in my nose, and join her.

"What was she doing?" asks Kat, her eyes wide now that she's here, at the spot of my sighting.

For a second, I think she's asking about Miss Carrera and her awkward attempts at one-armed brush-washing, then realize she's talking about my possible sighting of the ghost girl.

"Till yesterday, I didn't even know she *was* a she," I say, thinking of the Victorian victim of something-or-other that my classmates are so sure about. "But she wasn't doing anything really; just standing with her hand on the glass."

"Like this?" says Kat.

She places a hand on the window and affects a sad, lonely expression. With the sudden swoosh of violins soundtracking from the battered CD player, ripples of shivers run up and down my arms.

"And then she waved. . ." I say in hushed tones, the strangeness of that moment in my bedroom washing over me once again.

Now Kat waves – but in the sort of mad, flappy way little kids do.

She turns to me with a wide, giddy grin . . . and we both burst out laughing.

It was just a small, silly gesture that she did with her hand – just one of those dumb, daft, nothing-y moments between friends that crack you up – but it's like a dam's burst inside me.

It's been so long since I've had a friend to share dumb, daft, nothing-y moments with.

It's been so long since I've burst out laughing over small, silly stuff.

It feels so good to laugh till I cry that I don't care if the whole of the Art Club are staring.

And they are.

Ha!

*

"You look divine, Daddy dearest!" says Clem, glancing up from the homework she has spread over the small kitchen table.

"Well, I've had a shave and put a clean top on," he laughs, smoothing down the slightly wrinkly front of his three-button Fred Perry shirt.

"Do you want me to iron that for you?" I ask, wondering where the iron might be, since we're still surrounded by mounds of boxes. If we had any pet goats they'd be having a ball right now, in clambering heaven.

"Thanks, but I'm not *that* useless, Maisie!" says Dad, trying to smooth the creases out just a little more forcefully with his hands.

He is a bit.

I mean, he's great at lots of stuff. He's great at making food, helping with homework and handing out hugs. He's great at fixing broken things, remembering PE kits and recording stuff on TV that he thinks we'll like. He's great at being cheerful, even those times when he's probably not feeling cheerful inside.

He's just a bit useless at some of the domestic stuff, like ironing. When I was invited to Keira Murray's eighth birthday party, Dad left the iron on the back of my party dress so long that it melted the lace. It felt like I had an empty crisp packet under the cardie I wore on top to hide the mess.

He's not very good with bills either. He gets them, puts them in a purposeful pile, then loses the pile under stuff *just* long enough to risk the phone/gas/electricity being cut off.

He's also useless at telling us very much about Donna.

"So . . . is tonight the night?" Clem asks, her lazy cat's-eye stare fixed on Dad.

"Wh – what?" he stumbles, unsure what she means.

"Can you please – *finally* – arrange a date for us and Donna to get together?" says Clem, affecting weariness, though I know she's just as keen as I am to meet Dad's girlfriend.

"Maybe . . . well, maybe it's still too soon, eh?" he blusters.

"Six *days* is too soon, Dad. Six months is plenty," I jump in to point out.

"I know, I know – but let's not rush into anything," he says, agitatedly rubbing his head now.

"He's ashamed of us, Maisie," Clem says matter-of-factly, and turns back to her work.

"Hey, do you suppose he hasn't told her he has children?" I suggest, trying to keep a straight face.

Clem glances up at me as if she can see inside my head, sees the new lightness in there.

"Enough, enough!" says Dad, backing away from the double-trouble teasing. "See you later, girls. . ."

I follow him out, and watch as he goes down the path and through the iron gate in the tall railings.

"Have fun!" I call out after him.

Dad gives me a wave in reply, climbs into his car and slams the door shut.

I go to close the front door, then change my mind and lean against the frame, idly gazing at our battered silver Vauxhall Astra.

Dad knows and we know we're just fooling around with him, I think to myself as I stand there, but it IS starting to get kind of silly, how little we actually know about Donna.

In fact, here's all we've found out so far. . .

- Dad met her through a dating site.
- In the early days, Dad misled us. All the times he asked Clem to look after me because he was "having a pint" with a new friend called "Don"?

Well, he was actually in cafes, bars or at the cinema with *Donna*.

- Three months; that's how long Dad had been seeing her before he decided he really, really liked her and should really, really tell us that she existed (and wasn't a bloke called Don).
- He thought we might flip out at him when he made his announcement, and was completely surprised and blown away when Clem and me started shrieking and clapping our hands together like overexcited seals.
- She apparently has curly auburn hair, is very nice, and works in a doctor's surgery as a medical receptionist.

"Hey, don't be late – you've got school tomorrow!" I joke at the last minute, but Dad doesn't hear me – he's in the car with the window up – and the radio on, I bet.

Then – just before he drives off – he stops and rubs his face with both hands.

That's odd. . .

"Clem?" I say, going back into the house.

"Mmm?" she mumbles, sounding as uninterested as possible.

"You know that thing Dad does? When he's stressing?"

What I've just said makes her look up straightaway.

"What – the manic face-washing thing?" she asks.

"Yeah. He was doing it just now, in the car. He didn't know I was watching."

"Wonder what that's all about?" says Clem, leaning back in her chair and tucking her dark hair behind her ears.

"Can't be his job – he loves it," I reply. It's only Wednesday and he's already saying it's the best job he's ever had, with the staff and the students being so friendly.

"And it's not *this* dump," says Clem, wafting a hand around to indicate the cottage, "since he finds the place 'charming' for some unknown reason."

"We were talking about meeting Donna just before he left. . ." I point out, wandering if it's relevant.

Clem now rattles the top of her pencil between her teeth, like it'll help her think better.

"He knows I wouldn't be rude to her, right?" she finally says.

Wow. Is that almost an admission of guilt from

my sister? I wasn't sure she was even aware how rude she is on a daily basis to me and Dad. . .

"He knows," I reassure her. "We wouldn't be joking around with him if we felt weird about Donna, would we?"

I suddenly realize how nice it feels to say "we". There hasn't been a lot of "we" about me and Clem for years, and I miss it. Our only "we" times happen when we join together to tease Dad about his love life.

"Yeah, you're right," Clem says with a nod. (Now *that's* a phrase I don't hear from her very often, or *ever*.)

"Maybe he's just a bit tired," I suggest, pulling out a seat at the table and joining her, since it seems she's not going to growl at me to get out of her space.

"Or maybe things are rocky with him and Donna," says Clem.

"No!" I yelp. "Don't say that!"

Clem bursts out laughing at my shock and outrage. "Why do you sound so upset, Maisie? We don't even know the woman."

I blink for a second and try to figure out why I'm suddenly so disappointed at the idea of Dad and the mysterious Donna splitting up.

I guess part of it is that I've been excited for ages about the idea of meeting this person who's made Dad so happy (I've seen those smiles when her texts ping through).

And part of it is because Mum would be very, very proud of me and Clem managing to *Please stay open-minded if Dad meets someone new. . .* (Written halfway through the notebook, with a smiley face drawn beside it.)

"I just want Dad to be OK," I say, feeling the telltale prickle of tears threaten. There've been plenty of times that my heart's lurched at the thought of me and Clem leaving home for uni or whatever, and leaving him on his own. I can't stand it, and that's why I'd love our lovely dad to be loved by more people than just his kids.

"Yeah, yeah, whatever," Clem says gruffly, but she's passing me a tissue that she's found in her bag. "So . . . you haven't done your freaked-out zombie face for a day or so. School getting less awful?"

OK, my big sis is being halfway nice to me, but it doesn't seem like she's in the mood to handle a kid sister in tears, so I guess that's why she's changing the subject.

"Yeah, a bit," I say, blowing my nose and cheering

up at the thought of Kat. "I think I might have a friend."

"Yeah? A blind, deaf friend with no taste?" she jokes, but I can tell she's a little bit pleased for me. "What's her name?"

"Kat – with a 'K'."

"Uh-huh. And what's Kat-with-a-K like, then?"

"Well, she's not in my form class so we haven't had a chance to hang out *that* much yet," I begin, trying to remember if Kat said she was in 8T or 8G. "But she's really good fun, and I don't get the feeling she has a best friend at the moment. She's kind of different too – she's really pretty but has all this wavy, *big* hair that she ties back with a scarf like a headband, with a loose big bow here – sort of cute and cool, not like a little kid's bow, I mean. And today we spent lunchtime hanging out together at Art Club and—"

"Whoa!" says Clem, holding her hand up to stop me in my tracks. "Information overload!"

"Sorry," I say, realizing I've been gushing.

"It's OK," Clem replies, leaning back enough now to get her bare feet up on the table. "I guess it's kind of funny that I know more about your new friend in the space of ten seconds than Dad's girlfriend in all this time!"

I grin at her, and Clem grins back. Which feels good.

"So – without giving me a word-by-word account – what have you and Kat-with-a-K been chatting about?"

Her face gives nothing away, but I wonder if she's really asking me whether or not I've told Kat about what happened at my last school. Of course, I haven't, because a) there hasn't been time yet, and b) I don't know her well enough to mention something that might make her *well* wary of me. . .

"I dunno. Just stuff," I say, wondering if I should come out and tell Clem what we *have* been talking about.

"Hey, don't go coy on me! I've been thirteen too. Is Kat-with-a-K filling you in with all the gossip about everyone at school?"

Clem is so relaxed, so friendly, that I relax and feel friendly towards her too.

"Not really," I say. "It's just . . . well, there's supposed to be this ghost of a Victorian girl that haunts the school and me and Kat are thinking that we'll try and find out all about—"

"Nope! You know this sort of thing creeps me out," Clem interrupts sharply, her feet disappearing from the table, her hand back up in front of me in a very definite "stop". "Don't want to hear this, thanks!"

"But—" I try to continue, watching her fiddling with her headphones, ready to block me out.

"Maisie, it's bad enough that I have to live in this grotty, creepy dump, beside that spooky old school," she says firmly. "I don't want to hear any ghost stories. OK?"

I don't even get to say OK – or explain about the house not being creepy since Mr Butterfield didn't even die here – because the Arctic Monkeys are blaring and my sister's gaze is firmly back on her homework.

As I stare at her swinging bob, shutting her face off from me like a pair of brown velvet curtains, I think two things. . .

Our friendly, sisterly truce lasted about ten whole minutes.

And the ghost story that Clem doesn't want to hear? I'm not so sure it *is* just a story. . .

6

Always stay curious, never be bored or boring.

A celeb magazine is open on the table, with an argument raging above it.

"That is *hideous*," says Natasha, sticking her fingers down her throat and pretending to gag.

"You're joking, right?! It is *so* cool!" says Patience, shocked that Natasha doesn't share her taste in neon animal-print jumpsuits.

"Maisie – your turn for 'Choosies'!" says Rosie.

It's Thursday and it's Rosie and Bella's turn to be my minders today. Think they've been on a mission to find out more about me, but it's felt like an interrogation. Between classes, as they took me along corridors, up and down stairwells, it was questions, questions, endless questions about my old school, my old "friends". I mentioned Lilah and Jasneet, but didn't go into any details.

I swear I saw them sneaking knowing glances at each other a couple of times, and that doesn't make me feel too great. My old school might be on the other side of town, but what if someone knows someone who went there and Rosie and Bella are fishing for info, since they've heard what happened?

(Please, no!)

"What?" I say, not really paying attention to Rosie, not exactly sure what she's asking me now.

"Choosies," she repeats. "We all take turns choosing what we'd have off of these pages."

OK, I get it. I'm meant to look at all the stuff on this fashion spread and pick what I like best.

I try.

I look.

Natasha is right: the neon animal-print jumpsuit is horrible, but so is everything else.

Glancing up at the bundle of expectant faces staring at me, I worry about what to say. Is "none of them" an answer I can go with? Or should I just pick a hideous bag or top or necklace at random and hope it'll do?

The truth is, I can't concentrate on this dumb stuff – not when I have ghosts floating around in my head.

And then I see her, waving at me from the far side of the dining hall.

I'm saved. (Thanks, Kat.)

"Sorry – got to go," I say, grabbing my bag and excusing myself, trying *not* to feel the burning cold of eyes boring into the back of my head. . .

"*You* ask," I whisper to Kat.

"No, *you* ask," she whispers back.

"Please, *you* do it! You know the librarian," I say, my tummy twisting itself in a knot of shyness.

"Well, how will you get to know her if you don't talk to her?" asks Kat, with a cheeky lipglossed grin. "She doesn't bite!"

I hesitate, working up the courage to go on over and ask the librarian for the books we want.

Breathe, Maisie, I remind myself as I walk over to the desk with hesitant, birdlike steps.

"Hi," I say to the lady sorting books into what seem like random piles.

"Hello. Do I know you? Are you new?" she asks, lowering her head to peer at me over her glasses.

"Yes, I just started in Year 8 on Monday. I'm Maisie Mills," I tell her.

"Pleased to meet you, Maisie! I'm Mrs Gupta.

Now, if you can just fill in *this*, we'll get you sorted out with a library card in no time."

"Oh . . . right. . ." I mutter, thrown for a moment as Mrs Gupta passes me a ballpoint pen and a form. I glance at Kat, who has perched herself on a table by the window, one leg curled up underneath her.

"Go on – ask!" she mouths at me.

Easy for *Kat* to say, sitting there all comfy, watching me squirm.

But then again, my new friend does make me feel a little braver, somehow.

So . . . here we go.

I should just *do* it, *say* it, before time runs out, the bell trills and we have to get going to afternoon lessons.

"Um, I was wondering," I begin, as I scribble on my form, "do you have any books or leaflets about the history of Nightingale School?"

"Is it for a project?" asks Mrs Gupta. She's frowning a little. Probably because she knows what everyone in every year group is studying, and every project they've been assigned.

Or maybe it's because she can read my mind and knows that I'm scavenging around for anything about Victorian pupils meeting untimely deaths.

Thing is, Kat says we shouldn't ask straight out, and she's right. It doesn't take an A* genius to work out that schools don't like anyone dwelling on negative stuff connected with them, like bad exam results, mice in the kitchens, students who get expelled, or girls who die on the premises, in *any* century. And if I needed proof of that, I just have to remember Mrs Watson clamping right down on the ghost conversation in the dinner hall on Tuesday.

"I'm just interested," I say to Mrs Gupta, in a way I hope sounds convincing. "The school I've moved from was very modern and kind of boring. Nightingale seems so old and . . . and fascinating."

"Well, it's nice to find someone who's curious to learn about their school!" Mrs Gupta gushes, slipping out from behind her desk and waving me to follow her. "Most of the girls here are only in the library to go on Facebook – *even though they know they're not allowed to!*"

A few students look up shame-faced at Mrs Gupta's loud and pointed words; a few slink down behind their computer consoles.

I just go pink, knowing I've told a slightly white lie about my interest in the school's history. I'm pink, too, hearing Mrs Gupta praise me for my curiosity.

One of Mum's notes is, *Always be curious – never be bored or boring.*

Would she approve of me ghost-hunting? I don't know, and don't think it's the sort of thing I can ask Dad about.

I mean, it's not like, "What was her favourite colour?" or "Did she have any pets when she was little?" If I ask him, "Was Mum into the supernatural?" then he might think I'm going through a weird phase of missing her and am about to ask if we can do a séance or something.

"Here we are," says Mrs Gupta as she breezes past Kat, who is nibbling at her nails, but grinning at me too.

I half expect Mrs Gupta to do that teacher thing and tell Kat to get down off the table, but table-perching obviously comes low on the library's crime list after illegal Facebooking.

Mrs Gupta comes to a stop and reaches up to grab a slim leather-bound book from the top shelf. She passes it to me.

"Thank you," I say, remembering my manners, which I think is important when you're covering up for something you really shouldn't be doing.

"You're very welcome," says Mrs Gupta, swanning

back to her desk with an occasional glower at guilty-looking computer users.

"*She's* a bit fearsome!" I whisper to Kat.

"Mrs Gupta?" says Kat, arching her eyebrows at me as she slips off the table and on to a chair. "Hey, she is a total softie compared to Mr Holden. He used to go nuts at anyone who'd forgotten to do their maths homework. I mean, properly furious, like his *head* was going to explode!"

Kat pulls this mad face, looking like an insane, gurning, pop-eyed frog – and I have to slap a hand over my mouth to stop a snort of laughter escaping.

"Seriously!" she whispers, relaxing her face back into her usual infectious smile. "But the scarier he tried to be, the funnier we all thought it was. We called him The Grouch behind his back!"

So like me, Kat *did* have fun with her classmates once. What happened? When did it change? What made it change?

"Don't fancy landing in *his* class anytime soon," I mutter, grimacing.

"Oh, don't worry, he left ages ago," says Kat with a dismissive wave of her hand. "Anyway, come on, let's see what's in this book."

Fine, that's my cue to open *Nightingale School: A History*.

Me and Kat scan every musty, dusty page, taking about the same length of time to examine each photo, to skim all the words.

After a good long while, we turn to each other, thinking – I'm pretty sure – the same thing.

"Not exactly what we were looking for," I say, slightly overloaded with all the dry-as-dust facts and figures about various Victorian founders with handlebar moustaches.

"Kind of low on exciting stories of dead students," Kat jokes, ladling more gloss on to her already sheeny-shiny lips.

"So what should we try next?" I ask, looking down in disappointment at the stiff photos of the stern, long-ago gentlemen.

"Drawing glasses, cross eyes and blacked-out teeth on these guys?" suggests Kat – which makes me snort out loud this time.

"Hey, Maisie, what's so funny?" someone suddenly asks.

I glance up and see Patience staring down at me. She's got this heart-shaped, sweet face, skin so dark and smooth that you practically want to reach out and stroke it. But of course, that would be weird for two reasons . . .

1. she's looking at me like I'm bananas, and
2. it would be just weird, full stop.

OK, now that *last* thought has got me sniggering again. Kat drops her gaze to the table so Patience doesn't spot that she's doing the same.

Uh-oh: Patience – thinking I'm laughing at her – gives an irritated, embarrassed headshake and storms off.

"Ooo-OOO-oo! What's her problem?" giggles Kat, just as bad as me.

Help.

I know Patience will probably go running off to the others in our form class now, telling them that I've been giggling like a kid over some book with Kat; that I was weird or cheeky or whatever to her.

But it's like yesterday: I've spent so long on a laughter-free holiday that now it's started, I just can't stop.

"Hey," says Kat, her laughs fading down to giggles fading down to a happy smile. "This is fun, right?"

I have a friend.

A friend who likes me.

A friend who cracks me up.

A friend I can have an adventure with.

What could possibly spoil that?

A vague memory of best friends who turned into enemies flutters into my mind, but I swat it away, like a summer bug that wants to bite.

"Yes, yes it is!" I agree, wondering if we're talking about the ghost hunt or our shiny new friendship. . .

7

Don't keep secrets from each other.

I lie on my bed, my school shoes kicked off, flicking through an old photo album of Mum's from her teens.

We've got heaps of albums with Mum starring in them – just her and Dad, lots of Clem and me snuggling up to her as babies – but this one's my favourite.

Dad's told us a whole bunch of Stories About Your Mum based on this particular album, though it's just what he can remember her telling *him*, since they didn't get together till they were in their twenties. (Guess that makes them second-hand stories.)

"Your mum and her friends went to a youth-club disco every Saturday," I imagine Dad saying as I smile at the photo of my mum aged fourteen, arms around her gaggle of best mates. "She told me the disco lasted two hours, but the getting ready took three!"

I can see why: never mind the rah-rah skirts, leggings, ankle warmers and ribbons they were wearing, the smiling teenagers grinning back at me must have spent *for ever* backcombing their eighties hair, deciding which layers of bangles and necklaces to pile on.

I wish she'd kept some of her old clothes and jewellery from that time, I think, shivering slightly. It would've been fun to try them on, drape the necklaces and bracelets around me. See if I'd look in the mirror and recognize part of myself as that eighties version of Mum. . .

The shiver I felt: it's because a light late-spring breeze has meandered its way through the open window and is lazily blowing my curtains around, making them billow like the sails on some old-time galleon.

The billowing effect is 'cause my curtains from our old place are *way* too long for these small windows. They look kind of comical with those folds of material gathered on the ground, same as a clown wearing oversized trousers.

It would be good to take them up sometime; they do that service at the dry-cleaner's in town. But it'll wait; I'm not about to ask Dad, since I know there's a ton of stuff that needs fixing and sorting around here first, and it'll take him months of working and wages to be able to afford it all.

So, yeah, I'll wait.

Don't think Clem can, though.

"You know what I hate most about this place?" she said this morning, standing in her washed-out, faded dressing gown and latest foul mood, scowling at the too-slow toaster.

"No, but I think you're going to tell us!" said Dad, who probably wished he hadn't popped back for a minute to make a coffee for his flask mug.

"The carpet in my bedroom," Clem growled. "It's not just the ugliest thing I've ever seen, with that swirly pattern, but it's lethal too!"

I glanced up from my bowl of cereal, ready to make a jokey comment about her carpet carrying a gun, but then I remembered that this was Clem, who was pretty lethal herself in the mornings. Get on the wrong side of her and she'll cut you in two with her razor-sharp tongue.

"Dad, that thing is so threadbare, I caught my toe in a bald patch just now and nearly went flying!" she moaned on.

"Well, I'll make that top of the list of fixes when I get paid, OK?" he said wearily, heading out of the door, ready to do battle with the parents who liked to park on the zigzags if they could get away with it.

"*Don't keep secrets from each other*," I mutter now, watching the billowing curtains in my bedroom.

Another bit of advice from Mum's notebook, but advice I don't completely agree with. Like Clem's carpet woes; she could've kept them to herself for a bit, instead of giving poor Dad grief. And her loathing of the cottage; she really *should* keep that a secret.

With a sudden *whoosh!*, the curtains flap out into the room; long stripy arms reaching out for me. I place Mum's photo album down on the duvet and swing my legs off the bed, padding across my own tatty, faded carpet, thinking I should use the cream rope tie-backs that were left here by the previous family, when some other person lived in this room.

As I fiddle with the silky rope and hook, I gaze across the playground at the imposing red-brick school, at the three long windows of the art room, rising up from the roof terrace above the main entrance.

Three long windows with nothing in them except

the reflection of clouds flitting across the sky above our cottage.

I haven't seen the figure, the forgotten, century-old girl ghost, since Monday evening – if I ever saw her at all. And I have *tried* to spot her. Every day this week I've spent for ever at this window, gazing across, willing her to appear to me again.

Maybe that's the problem! Maybe she won't come if I stand and stare. Like a deer in the forest, perhaps she'll materialize when I'm not expecting it; I'll catch a fleeting glimpse of her out of the corner of my eye.

I'll do an experiment, I decide.

And so I quickly flip around and flatten my back against my bedroom wall, feeling the knobbles of the old-fashioned textured wallpaper through my thin school shirt.

One, two, three, four, five, I count silently to myself, then swivel around, hoping to see her suddenly there in the window.

No one, nothing.

I try again, giving it more time.

"One elephant, two elephant, three elephant. . ." I mutter out loud, pressed against the wall like an SAS officer ready to burst through the door of the bad guys' lair.

"Ahem!" comes a fake cough from the doorway.

"Dad!" I gasp, like I've been caught red-handed.

Caught searching for a girl who isn't there – but Dad doesn't know that.

"I *would* ask you what you're doing, Maisie, but I'm not sure I'd understand the answer!" Dad says with a wide grin.

"Just acting out a . . . thing we're doing in drama," I lie, hoping he hasn't looked at my week planner and seen that I don't have my first drama lesson till tomorrow.

"Harrumph," Dad snorts, not quite believing me, or just sniggering at how stupid I must've looked and sounded just now.

"And should I ask what *you're* doing here?" I say to him, checking my watch and seeing that it's nearly five-thirty p.m. "Don't you have buildings to inspect and doors to lock up about now?"

Yes, I'm using good-natured cheekiness to cover up my embarrassment and blatant fibbing.

"Just popped back for my phone – left it here earlier," he replies, holding up his battered black mobile.

In case of messages from Donna, I bet. He doesn't need his phone to stay in touch with me, since he can find me pretty easily, pretty quickly, any time of the day. It would only take a chat with Mahalia or June in the office, or a hover in one of the playgrounds at break time, to locate me.

And he's not expecting any messages from Clem, since she never sends any, or answers his, when she's busy at college or mooching with Bea or Marcus or Alima or one of her other friends.

"Did you have a nice time with Donna last night?" I remember to ask him, since I forgot this morning.

Dad's smile slips, just a little, then brightens again.

"Yes, thanks, honey," he says. "And hey, how are things going with that Kat girl you've hooked up with?"

Clem had told him about Kat. I bet his eyes lit up, hopeful that I'd found a proper friend, that things would work out for me.

"Good," I answer Dad, remembering me and Kat, our stifled sniggers in the library this lunchtime, at the same time as I'm wondering about that momentary disappearance of Dad's smile. What did that mean? *Is* Clem right? Could Dad be having problems with Donna? Does he have a secret of his own he's keeping from us?

"You should ask her around sometime," Dad chats on. "Invite her back after school one day, or at the weekend, maybe!"

After what went on at the old school, I know he's *so* desperate for me to have a new best friend that he'll probably bake a cake specially and put up a handmade "Welcome, Kat!!" banner above the front door.

"Yeah, I'll ask her," I say, just as hopeful and keen as he is, minus the cake and the banner bit, of course. Well, maybe the cake would be OK. . .

"Why don't you invite her soon? I could make my enchiladas for tea!"

"Maybe." I'm nodding, smiling, but joking aside, I don't want Dad to go overboard and scare Kat away. It would be like that time Ben Preston from two doors up in Park Close asked Clem to come to a gig 'cause he had a spare ticket. She thought it was all really casual, till he insisted on paying for everything, even bought her the band T-shirt afterwards when she nipped to the loo, and then tried to snog her at the bus stop when she was rummaging in her bag for her travel pass. She ended up calling him a freak and they ignored each other for the next year.

"Well, I'd better get going. The school won't lock itself up, will it?" Dad says brightly, stomping off down the stairs.

I have a sudden image of the phantom of Mr Butterfield, the previous site manager, creaking his way stiffly around the building, forever checking and rechecking that the doors and windows are locked.

"He's not even dead!" I mumble a reminder to myself, now starting to imagine spirits everywhere.

Whoosh!

The curtain that I haven't tethered yet flaps wildly, the noise of it making me start.

But as I quickly tie the runaway curtain back, I can hear a *new* noise . . . giggles.

I look out into the playground, but there's no one there except Dad, whistling his way towards the main entrance.

The soft sounds of giggles come again, not close, not far.

Hardly daring to breathe, I move towards the doorway of my room, and – like that game of Hot and Cold – I know I'm nearer to the noise.

"Getting hotter, getting hotter," I whisper, stepping out into the hall.

Clem's room.

It's where the giggles are coming from. They overlap, so I know that there's more than one person in there.

"Clem?" I call out, rapping softly at the door. When did she come back? I didn't notice she had; Dad didn't say.

Cold.

The giggles have stopped.

I push the door open and see an empty room; Clem's clothes on her rail-on-wheels, or strewn on the floor, possibly deliberately hiding the carpet she hates so much.

The buffeting breeze makes Clem's closed window rattle in its frame, and I jump all over again.

But it gives me a clue to what I heard . . . the wind carries sounds you wouldn't ordinarily hear, doesn't it? Well, there are flats over the back of the main playground. Behind that imposing red-brick wall, girls will be playing, laughing, and that laughter has swooped up and wafted over the bricks, over the rolling green of the grass, to my open window.

Yes, that's it.

There're sounds and smells, creaks and crackles,

ticks and tricks of the light to get used to in this new, very old, home of ours.

I go to close the door before my breath contaminates Clem's room and she accuses me of noseying in here when she gets home.

And then I see something out of the window that makes my heart lurch for the third time in as many minutes.

I re-cross the carpet, stepping on cast-aside clothes, and stare through the pane of glass at the school.

The long window on the left is open, when it wasn't before.

A figure in white is behind it.

And now the person is bending down, as if they're about to wriggle through the space, to come out on to the terrace. . .

8

Don't break rules – they're usually there for a pretty good reason.

Dad's mobile gives a chirpy little whistle.

It's the sort of noise that makes you smile, but this evening Dad is frowning as he glances down at it.

"Problem?" I ask, stuffing laundry into the washing machine.

"Um, not really, but. . ." he drifts off distractedly.

I know what the *but* means.

Last night I heard the whistle of an incoming text just as I walked into the kitchen to grab myself a glass of water.

Before Dad could leap up from the sofa and retrieve his phone, I had the quickest peek at the message on the screen.

Jack – would you be able to meet up tomorrow eve? Donna x

Yes, I admit that I peek at Donna's texts when I get the chance, which is really bad, I know, like reading someone's diary or something. But as it's my only clue to the person my dad likes most beyond me and Clem, I can't help myself.

Though I sort of wish I hadn't read *that* particular message. It was different from the others: cooler, with no smile to it. Maybe Clem really *is* right about things going wrong between them. . .

Then I spot Dad checking the clock on the kitchen shelf, right beside the framed photo of us all.

OK, so now I get it; I bet another reason for that *but* is the time.

"Dad, just *go*!" I tell him, straightening up and taking the wash basket he has balanced on his hip. "I'll finish up the laundry."

"But Clem. . ." he starts.

". . .will be back soon," I assure him. "She knows she's babysitting me. She won't be long."

"Yes, but I should still hang about till she's back."

"No, you shouldn't!" I tell him.

I don't want him to be late meeting Donna. I don't want any niggles between them. I want them to have as long as they need to chat about whatever they need to chat about and hopefully sort out their problems.

"But—"

"Dad, I'm thirteen. I can be left on my own for a while. I promise I won't play with matches, stick my fingers in plug sockets or invite axe-wielding maniacs into the house. OK?"

"OK," he laughs. "But are you sure you're all right to be here by yourself for a bit? After yesterday, I mean?"

Ah, yesterday. . .

I think I freaked him out, running out of the side door, across the empty playground, yelling for him at the top of my voice.

Then there he was – at the left-hand window of the art room.

He was reaching out to retrieve Miss Carrera's long white paint-splattered apron, which had somehow danced and twisted in the blusters of breeze and begun to flutter its way out of the open classroom window.

Dad caught it with one hand, then wriggled his way out on to the terrace so he could find out what was wrong – and talk me through the rational thing that had just happened.

Just a teacher's apron.

Just a fluke wind.

Just an open window.

No ghost.

Yes, of course; it all made sense.

This time.

(Though – and I'm not doubting what Dad said or did – wasn't that window *closed* when I was playing hide-and-seek at my window earlier, trying to catch the "ghost" out. . .?)

"I'm fine, honest, Dad," I tell him now, in our warm, cosy kitchen, even if a tiny bit of me isn't really.

"Right," he replies, nodding and checking his pockets for his wallet and car keys. "If you're sure we're all good, Maisie!"

"We're all good!" I say, jokily impatient with him, and giving him a playful push towards the front door. "Clem will get back any minute now. You'll probably pass her in the car."

"Probably," says Dad, leaning over to kiss me on the forehead – and then he's gone.

As soon as he is, I lean back on the kitchen units, idly staring at the happy family of four on the shelf by the clock, and phone the formerly sweet little girl who had her arms wrapped around her daddy's waist. The formerly sweet little girl who would do *anything* for her daddy.

"Clem," I say into my phone, just as soon as her answer message kicks in. "You've forgotten you're supposed to be looking after me tonight, haven't you?"

I leave it at that, because there's a ring at the doorbell.

It'll be Dad, forgetting something and wanting me to run back into the house and get it for him. Or Clem, with her keys lost in the depths of her slouch bag.

Opening the door, I have a smile ready for either of them, which wobbles slightly when I see who's *actually* standing on the pavement, outside the gate in the railings.

"Hi," I say shyly, hesitating before I go down the garden path towards her.

"Hi," says Kat, doing her funny little-kid wave, sounding just as shy as me.

It's like when you meet your teacher in the chemist, or your doctor in the swimming-pool changing rooms; the switch of location throws you.

Though me and Kat are hardly miles away from

school. The windows of it are watching us now, wondering what we're going to say, wondering why she's here.

"D'you want to come in?" I ask, releasing the lock and twisting open the thick black-metal door handle.

"Yeah . . . if that's OK?"

As I wave her into the garden, towards the house, it strikes me that we don't match. I'm in bare feet and leggings, baggy T-shirt and messy topknot; she's still neat and tidy in her school uniform.

My brain flashes to the time on the kitchen clock – seven forty-five p.m. Where's she been?

"I was passing, so I just thought I'd drop by say hello," she says, stepping into the cosy gloom of our hallway.

"That's great, of course," I reply, surprised and pleased, as I close the door. "Want a juice or something?"

"No, I'm fine," she says. "Hey, fancy giving me a guided tour, Maisie?"

Kat seems so different from the other girls I've got to know so far at Nightingale School: she's funnier, quirkier – and an outsider too, like me. But I guess she's the same when it comes to our cottage. Bella and

Natasha and Libby are all *dying* to see what it's like to live here, in the shadow of the school building, a house adrift on the ocean of the school grounds.

"Sure," I say, and point to the kitchen and the living room like I'm an air steward making passengers aware of the emergency exits.

Kat sticks her head into both rooms, commenting – I'm pleased to notice – on the things I like best in both.

"The jug by the clock is pretty. Love the colours!"

It's got this loud pattern all over it. Mum fell in love with it and bought it when she and Dad were touring round Spain one year, long before me and Clem came along. I wonder if Kat noticed the photo right beside it?

It would be nice to talk to her about Mum sometime.

"Ooh, that sofa looks comfy. It's all squashy like . . . like a giant marshmallow."

I'm kind of pleased she's noticed that too. When we were little, Clem and me would cuddle up on either side of Dad, lost in his arms and the fat cushions, cheering and booing the acts on *The X Factor*. Clem doesn't do that any more. If she ever joins us in the living room, she'll slump down on the beanbag, as if sitting in close proximity to us would bring her out in a rash.

I wonder if Kat'll stay a while?

Maybe I'll moan to her about Clem, as well as telling her about Mum.

I wonder if Kat has a sister?

But first question's first.

"So, where do you live, Kat?"

Kat takes a second or two to answer; she's too busy staring her way around the room, as if she's taking in every detail. "Me? Just a couple of streets away. Hawthorn Road. Do you know it?"

"No," I reply, wondering if I'll get a return invitation round there any time soon. "Don't know the area too well yet. What's your place like?"

"It's OK. Can I see your room now?" Kat asks, pointing upwards.

A ripple of uncertainty unsettles me. Not so much because Kat is already heading for the stairs, but because I get the feeling she doesn't want to talk about home. . .

"Um, it's probably a bit of a mess," I say apologetically, padding up the carpeted steps in her wake.

On the landing, she makes a mistake – a mistake

that gives me the chance to mention Clem.

"Is this it?" she says, pushing Clem's door open before I can warn her that we're in banned airspace.

"Nope – that's my big sister's room," I say, staying very much in the doorway.

"It's . . . nice!" Kat murmurs, treading on the threadbare swirly carpet and taking in the tatty patterned wallpaper, the purple duvet, the jumbled clothes rail, the make-up heaped on the dressing table. I suddenly feel unexpectedly sorry for my sister – Kat's wrong, it's not very nice at all. And this small, scrappy room really *is* a step down from Clem's bright, airy bedroom back in Park Close.

"My sister hates it!" I laugh.

"Really? It feels sort of . . . happy to me," says Kat.

She sounds so wistful it gets me wondering. I already have an idea that she's been lonely at school. Maybe Kat's home life isn't too perfect either. I mean, if she thinks this room is "nice" and "feels happy", what does that say about *her* house or flat?

Kat flops down on the bed, which makes me anxious – Clem's bound to spot any rumples in the duvet. Actually, it's completely rumpled anyway, so I brave it and flop down next to Kat as she gazes around.

"Have you got your own room, or do you have to share?" I ask, rootling for more info about her life and hoping I'm not being too obvious.

Now I'm right beside her, I can hear she's humming something to herself, but I can't make out what it is. Whatever, she stops to answer my question.

"I share with my little sister. I'm on the top bunk and she's on the bottom – singing or shouting, usually!" Kat laughs.

I laugh too. Then I notice a twinkle of tears in her eyes. . . Something *definitely* isn't right. I don't really know what to say or do, so I just suggest the first thing that pops into my mind.

"Er, my room's right next door. Want to see it?"

"Yes, please," Kat replies, quickly (and gratefully?) following me through.

"Ta-da!" I call out, throwing the door open.

"Wow, it's great," says Kat, glancing, nodding.

But weirdly, I can tell she's less taken with my room, even though – compared with my sister's – it looks more loved, with books on shelves, posters on the walls, clothes safely stored away instead of tossed on a clothes rail or on the ground.

Without taking much notice of my stuff, Kat walks straight over to the window.

Of course; she wants to look over at the art room from here. To imagine what I saw from this angle.

"So? See anything?" I ask, walking to Kat's side and staring out over the locked-tight long windows and the terrace in front.

"Nope, no sign of ghosts, or flapping aprons, even!" she jokes.

"Well, it IS Friday evening. Maybe the ghost has better things to do!" I say, and we both get a fit of the sniggers, as usual.

"Hey," Kat says suddenly, "are you here on your own?"

She's only just noticed?

"Yeah, my dad's on a date and my sister's hanging out with her friends somewhere, even though she's supposed to be home right now, looking after me!"

"And your mum?" she asks, opening her mouth to breathe on the windowpane and idly doodling a stick-man figure in the steam.

"Oh, she died when I was little," I say, shrugging.

"Oops, sorry," she says, wincing a little.

"Don't be. It happened a long time ago."

I'm sounding too casual, I know, but I tend to feel kind of self-conscious talking about Mum for the first time to people. It's like I'm more worried about making *them* feel OK with it or something. Like that matters more than the fact that it's mega-weird for me.

"So, what about you?" I charge on.

"What do you mean?" Kat asks, dotting eyes, nose and mouth on to her stick man.

Oops; *that* came out a little clunky. I sounded as if I was wondering if *her* mum had died too, rather than simply trying to change the subject and not doing it very well.

"It's just, I mean, how come you're here?" I say, with a nod to what Kat's wearing.

"Oh, that," she says, gazing down and realizing I'm wondering about her uniform, since school finished hours ago. "I had stuff to do after school. And I'm not in the mood to go home just yet."

"Why?" I ask, staring at her profile, her face suddenly pale and drawn and little-girlish in spite of the blusher and mascara and shiny lipgloss.

"I'm not exactly my mum's favourite person right now. . ." she says, marking what looks like the shape of a star round her stick figure as the steamy breath begins to fade away.

"Oh. I—"

Before I can take my turn saying sorry, before I get the chance to ask her what's happened, my mobile jangles into life in my back pocket.

"Hello?" I say to Clem, amazed and honoured that she broke her own rule of refusing to use her mobile to communicate with us.

"Before you give me a hard time, *yes*, I forgot. OK?" Clem snaps, as if *I'm* the one who's messed up.

"OK," I say, rolling my eyes, though neither Clem or Kat realizes. Kat is currently mooching around my room, checking out my stuff. She pauses and examines the photo of Mum and her teenage buddies in all their early Madonna-type finery that I took out of the album on a whim yesterday and propped up on my desk. It makes her smile, same as it does me.

"The thing is, I'm at Bea's," Clem rattles on, "so it'll be about half an hour till I can get back. Well, probably forty-five minutes; Bea's just trying out her new straighteners on my hair. But anyway, I'll be there *way* before Dad gets home. And no telling him – promise, Maisie?"

"Promise," I say, but she's already hung up on me.

"Problem?" Kat asks.

She may have been studying Mum's picture but her fingers, I notice, are resting on the rainbow-covered notebook right beside it. Kat has no idea how important that small, girly notebook is to me; those few stapled pages and the blue-inked words on them are my strongest connection to Mum.

(From what she said a minute ago, it doesn't sound like Kat has all that strong a connection to her *own* mum at the moment. . .)

"No – it's fine. Clem will be back in an hour," I say, recalculating my sister's promise to a more realistic time frame. When she's with her friends, minutes have a funny habit of becoming elastic.

"An hour, yeah?" says Kat, her eyes lighting up. "So . . . do you fancy doing something?"

She has a particular something in mind, I can tell. She's got a Cheshire Cat grin, only with added shimmer.

"Like what?" I ask, wondering why she's glancing outside at the playground, with its lengthening shadows and the warm, sepia glow of the evening sun.

"Like, *exploring*," says Kat, her face breaking into a wide daredevil grin.

I picture the silent playgrounds and sprawling empty lawn, dotted with clusters of cherry blossoms.

I picture the main school building, squat and waiting.

I picture the walk-in cupboard in the kitchen, where my dad's giant ring of keys is hanging up.

I picture opening Mum's notebook at a page that reads: *Don't break rules – they're usually there for a good reason.*

I picture snapping the notebook shut.

"Yes," I say to Kat, a matching grin spreading on my face. . .

9 Telling lies . . . it's not a good look.

"Wait!" I say, just as soon as my shaking hand has let us in the small side door of the school – the final door Dad shuts once he knows the building's secure.

The door happens to be right next to Dad's tiny office, which, I can't help noticing, still has Mr Butterfield's funny, old-fashioned name up on it. Maybe he hasn't got around to mentioning it to the ladies in the main school office yet. Or maybe Mahalia and June aren't as efficient as they like to make out. (Hey, they couldn't find my transition plan that first day.)

"What?" asks Kat, already halfway up the corridor.

"Listen – is there any bleeping?"

"What would be bleeping?" asks Kat, shining

the torch we took from the kitchen drawer into my eyes.

"An alarm!" I say urgently, blinking and protectively holding my hand up to mask the glare. "What I mean is, *is* there an alarm? Or, like, a keypad for one somewhere?"

I glance frantically around, and see nothing but a light switch on the cream-coloured wall. A switch that I'm not going to put on, since we don't want the nearby residents spotting the brightness and suspecting a burglar.

"Hey, I just remembered, there's a box in the front entrance," says Kat. "It's right by the office!"

We look at each other, frantically reading each other's minds.

"Run! Quick!" I yell, but Kat's already taken off, more sure of the twists and turns of the school halls and corridors than I am, since she's been here a lot longer than me.

The slap of our shoes on the tiled floors sounds incredibly loud, like it's being pumped through a sound system, with reverb added. It's so loud that I can't believe half the neighbourhood won't be able to hear it.

"Look – this is it!" pants Kat, as we hurtle out

of the gloom of the corridors into slightly brighter space of the main entrance hall, with its panels of glass around and above the double doors.

"Where?" I ask, panic and flying swathes of long hair temporarily blinding me.

"There," she insists, pointing to a wooden box to the left of the doors, to the right of the school office.

I kneel down beside it, looking for a way to open it, terrified of doing just that and seeing a neat row of numbered buttons, all flashing red for intruder.

Why am I so stupid? Even if this *is* the alarm panel, it's hardly going to have a great big idiot-proof "off" switch, is it?

"We won't know the code to disable it!" I splutter, my fingers still fiddling for a way to prise the cabinet open.

"We have to try, though," says Kat. "Look – a tiny keyhole. Is there a really small key on the ring to match?"

I fumble, but easily, almost magically, manage to find an *Alice in Wonderland* small key in amongst the larger ones.

"Here we go," I say, as the lock turns, the cabinet door opens, and we see. . .

"A letter box!" Kat giggles in relief. "It's just a fancy letter box!"

She's right; there are only a couple of hand-written envelopes in there, probably from parents, with cheques for lunch money or forms requesting holiday absences.

How dumb do I feel?

And if I hadn't been panicking so much the last few minutes, I'd have figured something *else* out. There wouldn't have been an alarm here in the front hall anyway, not if Dad – who's last to lock up – always leaves by the side door at the end of the day.

There is no bleeping, there is no alarm; the only sound is my heart thundering. Oh, and Kat's sniggers too.

"Come on – let's get on with the ghost hunt!" she says, taking the steps of the grand staircase two at a time.

Quickly getting my balance, I hurry after her, since a ghost hunt is what we gigglingly decide to call our "explore", and anyway, I definitely *don't* want to be left alone in the duskiness of the hall while the beam of our one torch disappears above me.

"Wait, Kat!" I hiss softly, though no one – except any elusive Victorian ghosts – can hear me.

"Hurry up!" Kat calls down to me, and I hear her wrestle with the brass door handle of the art room. "We'll need a key for this!"

And now here I am, panting at her side, fiddling for the right key under the spotlight of the torch that Kat's holding over my hands.

There it is; marked "A.R."

Job done.

We're in.

"SURPRISE!" Kat calls out, bursting into the room, her navy-blazered arms spread wide. "Aww, nobody here. . ."

"Yeah, well, if *I* was a lonely, dead schoolgirl wandering the corridors, *I* might just vanish at a noise like that!" I say, half jokily, half annoyed with Kat for potentially frightening away whoever might be here.

But hey, maybe she's just giddy and wild after the scare we had with the non-existent alarm.

(Non-existent alarms, non-existent ghosts. . . ?)

"Excuse me; may I have this dance?" Kat suddenly asks, rushing over to the dangling junk sculpture and grabbing it.

She starts singing a Spanish-sounding song I don't know and whirls the clinking, clanking artwork round as if it's her salsa partner.

"Careful!" I say, though I'm smiling at her silliness. "You might break it."

"It's all right; the *ghost'll* get the blame," Kat jokes. "Will you join us?"

"No," I laugh at her, instead aiming for the window sill just beyond, where I can park myself down and watch the sun begin its slow set over our cottage and the grounds and—

No!

It *can't* be!!

"Kat! We have to get out of here, NOW!!" I yelp, jumping off the window sill and lunging for the torch that's still in her hand, swirling a solo disco light on the ceiling as she dances.

"Why? What's wrong?" she asks, stepping away from her salsa partner, though it keeps jerking madly.

"It's Dad – he's just driving up to the house!"

I can recognize our car in the dusk, just by its sidelights alone; the right-hand-side bulb is faulty and always flickers.

Kat says nothing but follows me fast, wordlessly

taking the torch back when we get to the door so that my shaking hands can find the key and lock the art room door behind us.

Then we're off, trembling, baby-deer legs barely supporting us as we tumble down the grand staircase, along the zigzag of corridors, all the while hoping Dad's still too busy trying to find a parking space in the road to hear the echoing slap of our shoes as we try and beat him back to the house.

In a blur of unguessable seconds, we find ourselves in the cool of the evening, the door next to Dad's office closed, if not yet locked.

"Is it that one?" asks Kat, pointing to a key under the glare of the torchlight.

"No – that's not it. But here . . . *here* it is!"

Thunk.

The building is safely shut up; now we just need to get ourselves quickly to the cottage.

I left the side door open when we went out twenty minutes ago, and now the warm light just beyond it is like a beacon, welcoming us safely home.

Except a tall man-shaped silhouette is now standing in that same comforting pool of light, and my anxiety levels rocket skywards.

"Here," says Kat, grabbing the bunch of keys from

me with both hands cupped to muffle the noise.

"Hello, hello, what's going on here, then?" asks Dad, peering out at us, two figures bounding towards him in the softening light. "Been having fun, girls? Oh!"

I get what the "oh!" is. We've just come into view, our faces illuminated by the lamp on the hall table behind him, and he's expecting to see me and Clem, not me and a girl he doesn't know, her arms folded tight across her chest, as if she's terribly shy.

(*Please* don't let those keys jangle!)

"Dad, this is Kat."

And this is complicated, I fret silently to myself.

"Er, pleased to meet you, Kat," says Dad. "Didn't know Maisie was having you around tonight!"

"I just popped by," says Kat. "We've been sitting on the lawn, collecting fallen cherry blossoms."

Nice lie there, Kat, I think, though I realize it has to lead to another one.

"We, uh, dropped them . . . when I thought I heard the car," I quickly say.

"Well, fine, I suppose," says Dad, rubbing at his face a little, as he walks backwards in the hall, with us following. "Though *technically*, you're not really supposed to be using the premises without me, as a member of staff, being with you. It invalidates the insurance on the place, apparently. But, hey, I'll turn a blind eye to my daughter and her buddy sitting making daisy chains or whatever, just this once!"

"Thanks, Dad!" I smile at him, wondering what he'd think if he knew where we'd *actually* been, what we'd *actually* been doing.

Which I'm never, *ever* going to do again, by the way – my heart and my conscience couldn't take it.

The shock of how reckless I've – *we've* – been is sinking in and I'm shaking from the inside out.

And forget about the shock (I deserve that); telling Dad lies is the pits, mainly 'cause he's lovely and also because in Mum's notebook, she wrote, *Telling lies . . . it's not a good look*.

I'm probably not looking so good right now, with guilt-ridden eyes and a fake smile plastered on my face.

That's it; the lying stops *now*.

"Anyway, where's your sister?" asks Dad, stepping back to glance upstairs, for signs of life coming from her bedroom.

"She went to get ice cream for us," says Kat,

epically saving the day with a pulled-out-of-thin-air fib.

Though lying doesn't suit her either – Kat's all of a sudden paler than pale, her blusher sitting on her white cheeks like pink puddles on snow.

Before Dad can respond, the front door is flung open and Clem is there, surprise etched in her eyes as she finds herself being stared at by three people, one of whom she's never met.

"Hey, Clem," I jump in fast. "Didn't you manage to get the ice cream for us, then?"

Clem is super-sharp.

Clem can see I'm giving her a way out, a lie to cover her non-appearance as the babysitter.

She seamlessly joins in with us.

"Uh, no – the freezer in the shop was busted, so they'd all melted. Sorry!"

"No worries," I say with a shrug, my mouth so dry with lying that I can't say any more.

"Yeah, thanks for trying," Kat adds, as if she and Clem are old buddies.

"Whatever," Clem says back, acting ultra-friendly to this total stranger.

This is surreal. . .

"Well, that was a nice thought," says Dad,

wrapping an arm around Clem, obviously shocked and touched at her attempt at a big-sisterly good deed. "Still, if you dumb girls of mine had remembered, I picked up some ice cream *yesterday*, when I popped to Tesco. You even unpacked it, Maisie!"

Me, Clem and Kat all burst into slightly hysterical giggles at that, which bemuses Dad.

"Well, while you calm yourselves down, I'll go and get some ice cream for us all. . ."

"Not for me, thanks," says Kat, gathering herself together. "I have to go. I'll just grab something I left on your bed, Maisie."

She says it with a wink only *I* can see, which I figure is code for "I'll drop something key-shaped on your bed, Maisie". Great, and then I can smuggle them back on to their hook in the kitchen cupboard later.

"So, where do you live, Kat?" Dad asks as she comes tripping back downstairs again, her arms now by her side (with nothing to hide). "I could give you a lift."

"No, I'm fine, thanks," says Kat, continuing on towards the front door.

"But it wouldn't be any trouble, and it's starting to get properly dark now," Dad persists.

"Dad – leave her alone. You're freaking her out," Clem tells him.

Dad looks confused; frowns at Clem for more of an explanation. In the meantime, Kat fades away in the gloom of the hall, towards the still-open front door.

"Maisie's friend doesn't know you yet, does she?" Clem clarifies, giving Dad a lecture on adult/new friend etiquette. "She's not going to jump into a car with a total stranger!"

"Oh! But I was just. . . I'm sorry, Kat – I didn't mean to make you feel pressured or uncomfortable!" Dad apologizes, flustered now and rubbing a hand over his head.

"No, really, you didn't – it's OK," says Kat, backing out on to the path. "I live really close."

I follow after her, and let her out of the locked gate in the railings.

"That was scary!" I whisper to her through the bars once the gate closes behind her, the two of us talking like prisoners in neighbouring cells.

"It was kind of exciting, though, wasn't it?" Kat whispers back. "I haven't had that much fun in *years*. . ."

And with one of her little-kid waves, the night

swallows Kat up, her blazered figure darting in and out of the diffused yellow streetlamps that have just flickered on, till I can't see her any more.

Ambling back to the house, I feel a sudden rush of happiness. Kat really *is* my new best friend. Those shared, secretive conversations about families and friends . . . they *will* happen, and soon. The thought of that makes me a little scared but thrilled, thrilled that the weight of it all will lift off my shoulders at last. And Kat's too, hopefully. . .

And then I walk in on one last lie of the evening.

"How come you're back so early anyway, Dad?" Clem is asking, while digging a spoon into a small bowl piled high with raspberry ripple. "What went wrong with your date?"

"Nothing went *wrong*, Clem," Dad says defensively, which isn't like him. "It just wasn't quite a date tonight, just a quick chat."

"Ooh, a chat! *That* sounds ominous. . ." says Clem, waggling her spoon at Dad.

"It's not ominous . . . it's fine, really fine."

"Honest?" I ask, venturing into the kitchen.

"Honest," he says, passing me a bowl of ice cream. "Now scoot, you two; go find something for us to watch on telly. I'll just get myself some ice cream and be right out."

At the living-room door I glance back and see him rubbing his face with his hands.

Looks like Dad's just as good at lying as me and Clem.

We're a family of fibbers.

Sorry, Mum. . .

10

It's corny but true: a trouble shared is a trouble halved.

"You look lost, Maisie Mills!" says a cheerful voice.

It's Mrs Watson, trotting out of the double doors with an important-looking folder under her arm.

"I'm not lost; just trying to find someone," I tell her, moving out of the way as yet more girls lazily stream out of school, not in a particular rush to leave, even though the end-of-day bell went more than five minutes ago.

"Oh, yes? Got yourself a friend now?" she asks, interested and pleased for me. "Is it Patience? I *thought* you two would get on!"

Er, not quite. Now that they're relieved of their first-week-minder duties, Patience and the other girls in my form class have stepped away from me, just giving me the odd wave, a non-committal hello, an occasional sideways stare.

I really don't like the sideways stares.

It makes me think they definitely *do* know about what happened at my last school. . .

"Er, it's not anyone in my form class," I set Mrs Watson straight. "Her name's Kat. With a 'K'."

"Kat? You mean short for Katie Ross? Or Katherine Thomson? Or Kate-Lynne O'Malley?"

She fires those three names at me, plus a couple more, and I'm embarrassed to realize something.

"I don't know her last name," I say, pinking up.

"Oh, don't worry. It's early days! Lots to find out about each other, and plenty of time to do it in," says Mrs Watson, as she saunters off.

Well, Katie, Katherine or Kate-Lynne (or whichever she actually is) doesn't seem to have been at school today, or at least I didn't see her – and I certainly looked.

I looked for her on the lawn at break time, in the dinner hall at lunchtime. I hung out in the library, hoping she'd show, but only ended up leaving with a laminated library card, thanks to Mrs Gupta.

And call me impatient, but I want to find out everything about my new friend as soon as I can, even if Mrs Watson was waffling on there about having lots of time. (The thing is, I wasted too much time at my old school being miserable; I want to make up for it by being happy soon, *now*.)

I want to ask Kat a ton of questions, and I want to share lots of stuff with her too; stuff that's been sitting on my shoulders for months, crushing me.

The reason I feel so sure about it all today is because I went to bed early last night, with Mum.

Not with her tucking me in or reading me a story or asking if I'd brushed my teeth, of course.

Just me and her notebook, her words.

I'd been in such a blue mood, shocked at myself for going behind Dad's back and sneaking into the school, hating lying to him, that I lay there, letting my fingers trail back and forth across the rainbow, wishing I could take it all back, rewind a few hours.

But then guilt twanged in my chest, as I remembered what a buzz it had been to wander around the school all by ourselves, how Kat said she hadn't had so much fun in years. . .

Why hadn't she had so much fun in years, I found myself wondering.

It's corny but true: a trouble shared is a trouble halved, Mum had written on a page I'd kept coming back to last night.

I'd put down the notebook and walked over to the window, moving the curtain to one side. Softly, softly, I'd breathed on the spot where Kat had earlier – and a soft outline of a stick person in a star materialized. A stick *baby*, maybe, since it had a big head and tiny stick arms and legs.

"Let's halve our troubles," I'd whispered to Kat, wishing she could hear me, wherever she was.

And so I'd hoped to make a start today. To secure our friendship with a shared splurge of problems, of pasts.

But if Kat's off sick, I'll have to wait, frustrating as that is. . .

Hey, maybe I could at least find out which Kat she is? Didn't Mahalia from the office say she and June were the people to ask if I had any questions?

If they could look up today's registers for Year 8 and see which Kat (or Katie, or Katherine or Kate-Lynne) was ill today, I'd at least know my new friend's surname.

I walk back into the main entrance hall and join a queue of girls and parents at the desk of the reception, my hand covering the smile sneaking up on me when I catch sight of the "burglar alarm", i.e., wooden postbox.

What would people in the queue think if they knew I'd been in here on Friday night? Would they reckon it was funny? Scary? A bit wild? Maybe some of the parents would be outraged, think it was bad enough to be called to the attention of the head teacher, for the head teacher to rumble on about possible exclusions.

My smile slithers away at the thought, and memories of a different school, a different head teacher, different threats of exclusion creep unhappily into my mind. . .

"Hey, Maisie!" I suddenly hear Dad call to me, and see him struggling up the stairs with a stepladder and full bucket of soapy water. "Grab that for me, will you?"

I see a fat yellow sponge plopped down the stairs, an escapee from the bucket.

"Sure," I call back to him, suddenly glad to ditch the queue and my plan, since those dark, cloudy thoughts have drifted in.

"Thanks, honey," says Dad, pausing long enough for me to drop the sponge back in the bucket. "Miss Carrera's asked me to clean the windows in the art room – she says they haven't been done in months. Fancy keeping me company?"

"Sure," I say, biting my lip, and hoping Dad doesn't become instantly psychic. I don't want him picking up on my guilty vibes, or picturing me lurking in here on Friday, with Kat samba-ing and singing her funny Spanish-sounding song.

I grab the bucket from Dad, hoping to be helpful, trying not to grumble when the water splooshes down my leg, and follow him to my favourite room in the school.

"Oh, lovely!" says Miss Carrera, clapping her hands as we come in. "We'll have proper daylight in here at last. Oh, and hello, Maisie!"

"Hello," I say shyly, and hurry behind Dad like a duckling who doesn't want to stray too far from its mother.

As it's the end of the day, there are no students in here; just the art teacher in her long white cotton apron and the lilting sounds of classical music coming from her old, well-worn CD player.

"No problem. I'll get going on the outside straightaway," says Dad, opening the middle window wide and manoeuvring his ladder out on to the terrace.

"Can I come out there with you?" I ask him, intrigued by the outside space.

"Hmm . . . as the site manager, I have to say that's against health and safety regulations," he answers, as he props the ladder upright against the red-brick wall. "And as your father, I have to say no *way*; have you seen how low the wall is round this thing?"

The edge of the terrace is exactly like you'd imagine a castle wall to be: large, rectangular stones that go up and down, up and down, the lower ones reaching my mid-calf, by the looks of them, the higher ones not much taller than my knee.

"You can sit right there on the sill and chat to me, though, if you like," he says, reaching for the bucket and the sudsy sponge.

I perch on the ledge of the open middle window – one leg in the art room, one leg on the terrace – and watch as Dad climbs to the top of the ladder and begins cleaning the window where I saw, or didn't see, the ghost. . .

"So, Maisie, are we all good?" Dad asks, trotting out his usual remark, as he transforms the panes from dusty to damply clean in speedy sweeps of his arm.

It makes me think for a moment. I'd wanted to share my troubles with Kat today, and hear hers too.

But if she *isn't* around, I could *still* make use of Mum's advice, couldn't I?

“Yeah, I’m good, Dad,” I answer him as casually as I can. “How about you?”

“Can’t complain, he says, stepping down and down as the panes of glass gleam clear.

Here goes, I think, feeling strangely shy of asking my dad such a personal question.

“Uh-huh. But what’s going on with you and Donna?” I say, straight out, sitting on my hands to hide the fact that they’re shaking.

“There’s nothing—”

“And please, *please* don’t say nothing, Dad,” I cut him off, “’cause I *know* there is. . .”

Dad pauses, and stares down at me in surprise.

He’s still thinking of ways to brush off my words with some cheery, meaningless comment or other, isn’t he? But luckily, Dad’s so floored by my unexpected bluntness that he comes right on out with the truth.

“Uh, the thing is, I don’t really know what’s going on, Maisie,” he admits, stepping on to the relative solid ground of the terrace and scratching his tanned forehead.

“How come?” I ask, sorry that he’s not sounding more positive but quietly thrilled that he’s opening up to me.

"Well, when I saw Donna on Friday, she told me that . . . that she doesn't think it's going to work out – doesn't think *we're* going to work out," he says, now rubbing his face with the hand that (luckily) isn't holding the sponge.

"Why?" I ask.

"Don't know. She wouldn't – or couldn't – give me a reason."

That sounded strange. *And* unfair.

"Yeah, but what did *you* say to that, Dad?"

"I – I just asked her not to rush into any decision, and that's . . . well, that's how we've left it."

"But what do you think changed?" I say, as he turns and shuffles the ladder across to the window on the far side to me.

He storms to the top, carrying on the cleaning, only now going at twice the speed.

"I just don't know, honey," he says, not noticing that his frantic sponging is sending sprinkles of water and soapy bubbles cascading down. "For a while there, everything was going great. Then I got offered this job, and thought I'd lucked out. But it was around then that Donna went cool on me. Ha! How's *that* for timing, eh?"

You know, the other day, when me and Clem

were teasing him, I joked that Dad hadn't told her he had children. At the time I didn't believe for a second that was true. But it's worrying me now that maybe me and Clem *are* the issue, just by our very existence.

I mean, who in their right mind, however kind and friendly, would really want to take on two teenagers?

Hey, maybe I've just got to carry on being brave and ask Dad that too.

"Is it . . . us? Me and Clem, I mean?" I ask, clutching my knees to my chest, blinking as the warm drops shower down on me.

"No! I'm sure it's not, Maisie," says Dad, shaking his head. "Donna's always so interested when I talk about you and your sister."

Maybe she's just pretending, I think. *Or maybe she's just scared, now her and Dad are getting more serious, and* we're *getting more real*.

"So why don't you just ask her, straight out?" I suggest.

"I don't know. . ." Dad answers, shrugging, dripping. "I guess I'm worried that I won't like her answer."

Oh – so it's not just shy thirteen-year-olds who

are scared to ask deep and meaningful questions out loud?

"Well, if it was me, Dad, I'd rather know the truth than carry on wondering what was wrong," I tell him.

I did that with Lilah and Jasneet. The answer was awful, but the not-knowing was awful *and* frightening.

"But what if the problem is that she just isn't into me any more?" he asks, as if I'm an equal, a friend, and not his teenage daughter.

"Then it'll hurt, but it'll be her loss," I tell him.

"Well, I guess you're right, Maisie," says Dad, stopping suddenly and gazing down at me from the top of the ladder. "I'm just going to have to tell Donna I need the truth, even if I don't want to hear it. Thanks for helping me sort that one out in my head, honey."

"That's OK, Dad. *A trouble shared is a trouble halved*," I say, wondering if he'll recognize it as something Mum would've said. He doesn't seem to. "Do you want me to get you more water?"

"Yes, please," says Dad, and so I grab the bucket and slip inside the art room.

Fleetingly glancing back, I can see him looking

at me strangely, as if I just turned blue or grew an antler – or grew up in front of his very eyes.

I smile to myself for a second, then feel that instant, familiar flurry of shyness when I try to talk to the teacher.

"Miss Carrera, can I use the sink, please?" I ask timidly.

"Of course you can! And hey, Maisie, what do you say we perhaps play some music that's a little more upbeat now, while we tidy and clean, yes?"

"Um, yes, I guess. . ." I reply, trying not to spray water all over myself from the overenthusiastic taps.

A chirpy song bursts out as soon as Miss Carrera presses play on her tatty, paint-sploshed CD player.

"Don't you love it? It's called 'La Bamba'. It's kind of corny but it's one of those songs where you can't stand still when you hear it!" she laughs, dancing around as she carries on tidying away after the day's lessons.

"Hey, *I* know this one!" I exclaim, recognizing it from Friday, from the secret skulk around school. It was what Kat sang as she jigged around with the junk sculpture.

Miss Carrera spots me looking over at the artwork.

"Shh . . . don't tell anyone, but I've recycled this CD from that thing. One day, I just got the urge for something different to listen to, and there it was!"

"I won't tell," I assure her, suddenly giggling at the idea of the off-duty teacher sneaking up on the junk sculpture and snipping bits off.

"Now this I like! A little enthusiasm, Maisie Mills!" Miss Carrera says, laughter in her voice, salsa in her steps. "I don't want anyone to be shy around here. I think of this room as a sanctuary for all."

At her words, I forget about the song and wonder if I'm brave enough to ask her a question.

Go on, the brave part of me whispers in my ear. *It worked with Dad just now. . .*

"Miss Carrera," I begin, hiding my nerves by staring at the tap as I yank it anticlockwise, shutting the water off. "Do you know the story of the ghost that haunts Nightingale School?"

"Really? This place is supposed to be *haunted*? I only started here in January, so I don't know all the school stories yet," says Miss Carrera, amused rather than intrigued by what I've just said. "What's it supposed to look like?"

"It's a schoolgirl, from Victorian times, when the school was first built," I tell her. "In fact, it's mostly been spotted in here. . ."

By *me*, I don't add.

"In here? My, my!" says Miss Carrera, most definitely delighted rather than terrified at the news. "But wait; actually, now you mention it, Maisie, I think I *did* hear something in the staffroom once about a tragedy of some kind. . ."

She blinks hard, as if she's flicking quickly through a box of files in her memory.

I hold my breath – as well as the sloshing bucket of water – hoping against hope that she can remember, that she can give me some sort of clue that Kat and I can work with.

"Hold on, now I remember . . . it wasn't a student," she finally says.

"What do you mean?"

"It was some kind of an incident. . . I don't know what it was exactly, but something *bad* happened to the previous site manager. The older man who was here before your father."

Mr Butterfield? But that doesn't match up with

the ghost story Hannah and Patience and everyone told me, I realize. My heart, my stomach, even the arm holding the heavy bucket all sink with disappointment.

But what "bad" thing had happened to Mr Butterfield, I wonder. . .

"Sorry, Maisie – how useless am I? I haven't been of any help with the exciting ghost story, have I?" Miss Carrera laughs, bursting into my thoughts. "Now show me: where exactly is this little ghost girl meant to appear?"

"Over there, by that window," I tell her, pointing to the gleaming, glass-twinkling window beyond the junk sculpture.

"Well, you know, I *hate* to disappoint you, Maisie, but I'm in here on my own a lot, and I've seen no trace of spirit girls from the late 1800s or whenever," she says, hands on hips, blowing a stray wisp of hair from her face. "All *I've* seen is are the traces of greasy fingers made by twenty-first century girls! So can you ask your dad to do me a very big favour and clean the inside of the windows too?"

As I make my wobbly way over with the refilled bucket of water, I see what Miss Carrera is getting at; there are fingermarks aplenty on the glass, from all the girls who sit here at Wednesday Art Club probably, chatting and staring out of the window instead of working.

And with a gleam of sun on the glass, I make out one smudged shape in particular. . . A pointed edge. Several points, in fact. A squidgy star, a stick baby in the middle of it.

I smile to myself, almost feeling Kat's presence, even if she isn't here today. I imagine her breathing on the glass, doing her little doodle, before salsa-ing off to the Spanish sounds of Miss Carrera's (stolen) CD.

I'm so glad she's my friend.

"Wait till I tell you what I just found out!" I whisper to Kat's stick figure, since it'll have to do till I next see her.

And like Mrs Watson said, we've got all the time in the world. . .

11 Always trust your instincts.

There IS a ghost.

No, there isn't.

There IS a ghost.

No, there isn't.

I'm in the dilapidated summerhouse, in our dilapidated garden. It's the first time I've properly ventured out here, rather than just peering at it from the house, but Clem's been doing my head in ever since she got home from college. She's been playing her horrible drum and bass music so loud I couldn't stand it.

I couldn't stand hearing it booming in my room-next-door-to-hers.

I couldn't stand it thumping and thundering everywhere I went in the cottage.

I couldn't stand it that she kept saying "Sorry,

what? You want me to turn it *up*?" every time I tried to ask her to *please* turn it down.

So until Dad finishes up at school, I'm planning on hiding out here, and it's turned out to be pretty nice so far, if you just ignore the nettles on the way in and the scuttling bugs once you've made it inside.

There IS a ghost.

No, there isn't.

There IS a ghost.

No, there isn't.

The reason those words are wafting through my head is 'cause I don't trust my instincts one bit, which might disappoint Mum – if she was in a position to know what was going on with my life, that is.

But who could blame me? I thought I'd always be able to rely on Lilah and Jasneet, and look how wrong I got that. I thought Saffy seemed like fun, and it turned out she was the *opposite* of fun.

So when it comes to figuring out if a ghost haunts Nightingale School, or if there's a reasonable, rational explanation for what I've seen, I think I've got a better chance of getting the right answer by sitting here in the tatty summerhouse plucking petals off this flower in my hand than trusting my useless instincts.

And maybe my current edge-of-grouchy mood is down to the fact that I'm slightly disillusioned after Miss Carrera laughed off the idea of any unusual, out-of-the-ordinary schoolgirls materializing in her art room when I spoke to her an hour or so ago. (My instincts were pretty off-kilter when I decided to talk to her too, I guess. . .)

"Oi, Maisie! Visitor!" Clem suddenly barks from the back door of our house before instantly walking straight inside again.

Wow, my big sister is quite the hostess. (Not.)

Then when I see who she's left standing marooned on the small, mossy patio, I quickly stand up from my daydreaming and petal-plucking.

"Hi!" says Kat, giving me one of her funny little-kid waves. "Should I come over to you?"

"Sure," I say, scrunching up the half-bald rose I've been idly fooling around with and chucking it out of the window of the summerhouse (easy – there's no glass in it).

Hey, Kat's in her school uniform . . . which I guess wouldn't be so surprising if she'd actually made it into school today. Or did she, and I just didn't see her? Unless she was avoiding me for some reason. That happened a lot at my old school.

My sudden paranoia makes me bumbling and shy.

"Just watch out for the nettles," I call out, slipping Mum's notebook into the big pocket of the baggy cardie I changed into once I got home.

"How cool is it to have this in your garden?" says Kat, pulling at the summerhouse door to open it.

Then realizing it's jammed but has no glass in it, she simply steps in through the gap instead and joins me.

"It's great, isn't it?" I agree, warming up a little now I see her smile. "I'm going to ask my dad if he can fix it up a bit. Then I could paint the whole thing, stick some cushions and stuff in here, and have it as my special place."

As I chatter and Kat sits, I notice the dark rings under her eyes. . . She doesn't look a hundred per cent well. She *must've* been off. Wonder what's been up with her today? I'll ask in a second, once my stupid shyness fades properly.

"Sounds good. I'd love to see it *returned to its*

former glory," says Kat, fooling around with a fake posh voice, and a flourish of one hand.

"I could have an opening ceremony when it's done," I fool around back. "With a red ribbon to cut and fancy canapés and stuff."

I hold my hand up, sticking my pinkie in the air.

"Sounds very fancy," laughs Kat. "Would I be invited?"

"Why, of *course* you'd be invited," I reply. "You'd be my guest of honour."

A small jangle goes off somewhere inside my head, alerting me to the fact that Kat might not have been ill; maybe she was absent because of something to do with her family, her mum, even? But I know that jangle is just my instincts talking, *jabbering* more like, and we all know how unreliable *they* are. . .

"Ooh, your guest of honour? That would be fun," Kat says, her eyes taking in every nook and cranny of this old, glorified shed as she settles herself cross-legged on the creaky, built-in box bench. "Hey, and you could always invite your *old* friends here, once it's all done up."

"I don't have any old friends to invite."

Well, *that* came out nice and bluntly, with no sugar on top.

"How come?" asks Kat, her fingers running over the summerhouse's rough weather-battered surfaces, nails picking at loose paint and wood.

So, is this it?

Is this when I come out and tell her?

Well, I guess it's been a day of being brave. An hour ago I asked Dad about Donna, told Miss Carrera about the ghost.

It's time to act like a diver, teetering on the top board at the swimming pool. It's time to dive in. . .

"I got in a mess at my last school," I begin, curling my legs up underneath me, to make myself smaller, as if I'm a target.

"Yeah? What kind of mess?" Kat asks, interested but not all super-keen, as if she's sniffing for gossip.

"I had these best friends, Lilah and Jasneet. I mean, for *years* they were my best friends, ever since primary school. And then this new girl called Saffy Price arrived, and she started hanging out with us."

Kat tilts her head as she listens, her silky hair bow flopping to one side. "Hmm, let me guess. . ." she says with a sympathetic smile. "It didn't go well?"

"It did for a while," I tell her. "Saffy seemed pretty good fun. It felt like she fitted in with the three of us."

"There's a big fat *but* coming, isn't there?"

It makes me more confident in telling my story, knowing Kat saw that *but* coming a mile away.

"Uh-huh," I say with a heavy nod.

"*Knew* it," says Kat, clapping her hands together. "I don't like this Saffy already. Go on – tell me what happened. What was the *but*?"

"*But* I kind of started to suss out that Saffy maybe wanted Lilah and Jasneet to herself," I carry on, biting nervously at my thumbnail. "She began making all these snippy little comments, taking offence at things I was saying, even if I hadn't meant anything at all."

"OK, now I *really* don't like her," Kat bursts out, with a mix of jokey protectiveness that I really appreciate. She slaps her palms down on the built-in bench for emphasis, but it's so old and crumbly that I hear something go *crack*.

"It's all right, just a sort of lid thing has come loose. Nothing broken," she says, trying to press a raised bit of wood back into place. "Carry on."

And I do, since I've got this far.

"Honestly, for a long time, I didn't want to believe that Saffy was slowly turning Lilah and Jasneet against me," I say. "Then all of a sudden, I knew for sure."

"Yeah? How come?" asks Kat, still listening intently – though now her fingers seem to be trying to prise the lid in the seat open.

"It was at the school fireworks party," I say, watching as Kat's hand rootles around in the space below the now-opened lid.

Is she even listening to me properly?

"Go on," Kat looks up and urges me, so I guess she is.

"We were allowed sparklers, if we were careful. *I* was careful, but Saffy was mucking around and giggling with Jasneet and Lilah, and somehow she fell back into me. . ."

I crumple into myself, the memory of the moment too awful to bear.

"What happened?" I hear Kat ask, much more softly now, no jokiness in her voice anymore.

The words stick in my throat like small, jaggedy stones.

"I hurt her," I mumble in the tiniest of voices.

"You did *what*, Maisie?" Kat asks, struggling to hear me.

"I hurt her!" I say louder, lifting my head, the truth jarring my throat as the stones scrape and scratch. "I burned her face!"

"Hey, hold on. It's not like you *meant* to do it," says Kat sharply. "You just told me; you were holding a sparkler, right? And that Saffy girl *fell* – which makes it an accident. Accidents are horrible, but they happen, Maisie. It's *not* your fault."

Her voice suddenly has a wobble in it, as if she's angry and hurt on my behalf.

"Try telling everyone *else* that," I mutter darkly, remembering the horrible scream coming from Saffy, the gut-churning fear that I'd blinded her, the ambulance siren shrieking closer through the dark and the crowds and the chaos.

"So what happened next?" asks Kat.

"The head teacher told Dad it would be best if he took me home," I say, sorrowfully. "The next morning I ran up to Lilah and Jasneet at school, asking if they'd heard how Saffy was. But they were so weird; they just shrugged and looked at each other. I had to force them to say what they were trying *not* to say."

"Yeah? And did they say in the end?"

"Uh-huh. They accused me of deliberately burning Saffy. . ." I tell Kat, wincing at the memory. "Even the head teacher believed that's what happened, 'cause that's what Saffy told him. Same went for Lilah and Jasneet, since Saffy convinced them it was the truth."

"So, Saffy must have gone away and thought about it, and realized the accident was a good way for her to get everyone mad at you – and on her side?" Kat suggests.

"Yeah, that's about it," I say, realizing I'm rubbing my hands over my face the way Dad does when he's stressed. "I got excluded for a week."

"Excluded? Like, *banned* from school?"

"Uh-huh," I mumble.

What a week that was. I don't think I stopped crying the whole time. In fact, I cried so much that Dad worried I'd get dehydrated, and kept forcing me to drink glasses of water, when he wasn't busy comforting me, or on the phone, trying to get the head teacher to reconsider. (He didn't.)

I remember that my mild-mannered dad got so worked up that he was determined to go charging around to Saffy's, to demand a meeting with her parents. "Then once she admits to them that she lied, I'll phone Lilah and Jasneet's parents, and set the record straight!"

Poor Dad had his jacket on, his car keys in his hand, red rage in his eyes. It took me begging him not to do it – and Clem pointing out that Saffy's parents might get the police involved – to get him to back off.

And so we just waited out the week, crying (me) and hugging (him).

"How did it feel, going back to school after that?" I hear Kat ask, since my head is now somehow buried under my baggy cardie.

"I *so* didn't want to go in and face everybody," I mumble into the woolly material, "but Dad said I *had* to, or people would think I really did have something to be ashamed of, or that I *was* to blame."

"Wow. That must have been tough."

"Worse than tough. It was seriously *bad*. People thought I was to blame anyway. No one talked to me any more; not a single person. And then I saw Saffy for the first time and she had the *tiniest* scar on her cheek – like a spot! You wouldn't even have known anything had happened to her."

The scar inside me – caused by not being believed – was much, *much* bigger, and *still* hadn't healed.

"Hey, it's over," says Kat, suddenly sounding nearer.

I glance up slowly like a tortoise peering out of its shell and see that she's on her knees in front of me. She grabs one of my hands in hers.

"You're safe and you're *here*, Maisie; *you* know the truth. Don't let it linger."

Don't let it *linger*?

My life has been ruined by an accident that someone turned to her advantage.

"Don't let it linger" is what you say about bad smells. Saffy Price is much *more* than a bad smell, she's. . .

Actually, you know something?

Comparing her to a bad smell is kind of fitting when I think about it. And what Kat says is true: she isn't around any more, poisoning the atmosphere.

My life is here at Nightingale School now, and the scents of the cherry blossom trees and the lawn Dad just cut are in the air and filling my senses. . .

"Want to see what's in the box?"

What?

Slightly flustered, I notice that while Kat is still holding one of my hands in hers, in the other she's grasping a slightly rusty-looking shortbread tin, complete with cutesie Scottie and Westie dogs on the front.

Is that it? I've lugged around the pain of what happened at my last school for all these months and now the conversation is closed, just like that?

No more stressing over the unfairness, the lack of loyalty, the finger-pointing, the shunning.

It can't just vanish because I want it to.

Can it?

Can it?!

A sudden smile plays at my lips.

What are the rules?

Are there any rules?

Is there a time limit for my misery, or can I just ditch it now, like a rucksack full of bricks, and walk away?

"Yes," I say to Kat, staring at the tin box, feeling suddenly floatily light, like someone's turned up the brightness inside this shady summerhouse. "Let's open it."

"It was in there," says Kat, nodding back at the bench and the hidden compartment in it.

She prises the reluctant tin lid open with a creaky pop, and we see a collection of faded pieces of paper.

Top Ten Singles – 1987 says one that seems to be torn out of a magazine. A list of songs and artists is underneath the heading, but I'm too curious to see what else is in the box to read any more.

"Take a look at all this. . ." says Kat, passing me the sort of small plastic comb you wear in your hair when it's piled up. "Isn't it great?"

I nod, examining a glass pot of iridescent blue eyeshadow; a pair of lacy, fingerless gloves; a snipped-out picture of a younger version of that old pop star Madonna. Just the sort of stuff my teenage mum and her friends would've been into, back in the eighties.

"It's like a time capsule!" I gasp, spreading out the bits and bobs on the bench next to me. "And look at this – it's a postcard addressed to someone called Lindsey Butterfield. She must've been the old site manager's daughter!"

I'm not sure if Kat is paying any attention to what I'm saying.

She's too busy with what looks like a school photo.

While she stares down at the image of the students, I gently pull the photo up, so I can read the writing I've just spotted on the back.

Names – scribbled names of girls.

Girls' names like Lindsey.

Other names in a row like Joanne, Laura, Sharon and Anne.

Names that aren't so common now, and that's no surprise, since at the top it says *Class 8G, 1987*.

My eyes scan the bottom row of names.

Pamela, Jenny, Suzanne and Katherine. . .

Kat makes a sound like a little whimper, and I glance up at her.

Uh-oh: she really doesn't look well, and I've forgotten to ask what was wrong with her today.

"Hey, are you feeling OK?"

I might have asked the question, but I don't think I'll hear Kat's answer, even if she gets around to saying it.

'Cause she's flipping the photo around for me to see.

A photo of smiling, cheery girls in navy uniforms,

posed in descending rows outside the stern façade of Nightingale School.

Girls with hairstyles that are large and puffy, girls who are wearing just a *little* too much make-up, since that was the fashion in the 1980s.

And in the front row, to the left, there's a face that's somehow familiar – or maybe it's the bow in the hair that does it.

The girl's face is friendly, the smile warm, the lipgloss shimmery.

Her expression is full of life . . . which makes it all the more shocking to see the circle of black pen around her head, and the letters *R.I.P. x* beside it.

I flip the photo over, my eyes scanning the names, working out which girl this is.

And there it is. The matching name.

I flip the photo back and forth a few times, just to make sure that what my eyes are telling me, what I realize my instincts are *screaming* at me, is right.

"Katherine," I say out loud, looking directly at the girl kneeling in front of me.

The girl who looks exactly like the person in the picture.

"Hello," she says nervously, biting her sheeny-shiny lip. . .

Treasure your old friends, and be open to making new ones!

"You're dead."

It's not the nicest thing you can say to a friend, but I can't think of any other way to phrase it right now.

"Mmm." Kat nods, biting her nails, watching me, trying to gauge how I'm going to react.

Actually, I think I might faint.

But then again, I think I may throw up before that.

Kat suddenly sees I'm struggling with this new, shocking situation and touches me gently on the knee. That soft touch does something strange but wonderful . . . it's as if the finest, flimsiest puffs of cooling air brush the whole of my skin, and my temperature – and anxiety levels – come down a notch or two, taking me below the point of fainting and throwing up, below the point of my heart beating out of my chest in panic, below *normal* even, to long-distance swimmer calm.

Kat . . . somehow *Kat's* making this happen, I know it.

But at the same time, she's growing paler, the dark circles more obvious under her eyes, the pink-brown blusher sitting on her cheeks like the paint on the face of an antique porcelain doll.

And now her huge blue mascara-fringed eyes are staring up into mine, as if she's begging me to be all right with . . . with whatever this is.

I know she's waiting nervously for me to say something.

And despite my sudden slow and relaxed heartbeat, I have *so* many questions ramming and crashing around in my head that I'm finding it hard to figure out which one to ask first.

I think I just have to open my mouth and take a chance with whatever comes out.

"What?" I end up saying, pretty stupidly.

"Huh?" Kat frowns.

I guess dead-girl ghosts have many, varied and *amazing* powers which I can barely guess at, but perhaps trying to figure out quite what I'm on about with that one useless word is optimistic, really.

"I mean . . . what *are* you?" I stumble. "Are you an actual, real-life ghost?"

OK, that sounds dumb too.

But Kat has seemed really, really *real* to me since I first met her, since she linked her flesh-and-bone arm in mine that lunchtime in the hall, last Tuesday.

"I can feel alive, *seem* totally alive whenever I want to, if I concentrate," she tells me now, looking half-dead, she's so very, very pale all of a sudden. "I just can't do it too often, 'cause it takes all of my energy, and it can take me a long time to get back."

"But . . . what does that *mean*?" I beg her, desperate to understand. "Get back from where?"

Wherever it is, I'm guessing it's where she's been today.

"Nowhere," she shrugs. "I just feel exhausted and it's like I fade away to . . . well, nothing. Then I start to feel stronger, and I'm back, hovering around the school again."

"How does that work? How do you explain why you're there one day and not another?"

"It's not like that, Maisie. I've chosen to appear real to you and your family," says Kat, her eyes getting bigger and more earnest as her skin grows whiter. "But the girls and the teachers at school don't really see me – not properly, anyway."

"So . . . so you're *not* in class 8G?" I ask, still battling to sort my millions of questions into some sort of sensible order.

"Well, I *was*, back in 1987. Now, I just drift in and out of the crowds in the corridors. Sometimes a person will sense me. A girl maybe shivers when I pass, or sees the shift of where I've been."

"The shift?" I repeat, though my brain is busy trying to compute the fact that neither Mrs Gupta or Patience actually saw Kat in the library that lunchtime last week – and there I was, thinking they were just ignoring her.

"You know how sometimes think you see a movement out of the corner of your eye, but then you look and nothing's there?" says Kat.

"Yeah, sort of," I say with a nod.

"Well, that's the shift."

"Right," I reply, feeling a ripple of goosebumps on my arms. "So when you get that feeling, it usually *is* something?"

Kat tilts her head to one side and smiles at me. "Yes, it usually is," she laughs ruefully.

I guess that makes sense. Well, as much sense as

having a dead best friend *can* make sense.

Then a specific question urgently shuffles to the front of the queue, demanding to be asked.

"What . . . what happened to you, Kat?"

I hold up the photo, pointing to her image, to the *R.I.P. x* beside the circle of black felt pen ringed around her face, in that happy row of long-ago girls.

"I don't know," says Kat, blinking up at me. "All these years I've had these jumbled flashes and glimpses of what my life was like. But I've never seen anything about my death. And I *have* to know, Maisie, or I'll just go on and on like this for ever. . ."

At that moment, *another* specific question shuffles to the front of the queue in my overheating head.

"You think *I* can help?" I ask, the truth dawning on me.

"Yes!" Kat says, nodding enthusiastically. "As soon as I saw you I felt *so* sure you could."

"But why?"

"Well, that's a stupid question!" Kat laughs now, sounding like any normal, non-dead teenage girl. "I knew you had to be special. You were looking *straight at me.* You were the first person ever who could really, clearly see me!"

"On Tuesday, in the dinner hall, you mean?" I say, visualizing all the girls gathered around me, telling me about the Victorian ghost. Kat came to talk to me as the huddle of girls broke up at the sound of the bell.

"No . . . it was *before* that," Kat surprises me by saying.

"Before?"

"Yeah, it was when I knew that *you* saw *me*," she grins. "It was when you looked out of your bedroom window for the first time. Remember?"

How could I forget?

She's talking about the Saturday before last.

The day we moved in.

The art room window.

Of course; in the muddle of my mind I suddenly get what's blindingly obvious: there *is* no Victorian ghost.

There is no Victorian ghost, because the only ghost is Kat.

The long-dead, century-old schoolgirl . . . it's just been a fairy story all along, a myth that's drifted like a Mexican wave through year upon year of students here at Nightingale School. Students who sensed, saw or felt Kat's presence over the decades and imagined and explained her away as some sort of fictional, floating spirit, a ghostly character that wouldn't look out of place in a Charles Dickens novel. . .

So the shape I saw at the art room window, the shape Dad explained away as sunlight hitting the window; a reflection of a cloud or a plane; the outline of a twirling junk sculpture (the vision of "dead" Mr Butterfield, if you were listening to Clem), all along it was this not-so-ordinary girl crouched in front of me now.

"Kat, when me and my dad came to look around the school that Saturday afternoon . . . was it *you* making the junk sculpture twirl when we were leaving the art room?" I ask.

"Er, yes," Kat says apologetically. "I was just trying to get your attention."

Get my attention? At the time it got me shivering up and down my back, wondering if I was going a tiny bit mad.

"And then last Monday – it was *you* waving back to me from the window?" I check, knowing even without asking that it was no cleaner or Miss Carrera that day. (I think I knew already.)

"Uh-huh."

And Miss Carrera on Wednesday lunchtime; she saw only *me* coming in for Art Club, didn't she? Same as the rest of the girls there saw only *me* burst out laughing on my own, while I'd thought I was goofing around with my friend. My friend who wasn't there.

"On Thursday . . . was that *you* opening the window and stepping out on to the terrace?" I ask, thinking of Dad grabbing the flyaway white art apron belonging to Miss Carrera.

"I *think* so," says Kat, frowning now, looking unsure, looking like her skin is becoming semi-transparent (the veins in her forehead are very, very visible; very, very blue).

"Why do you only *think* so?" I push her.

"I don't understand it all, Maisie. Sometimes I can control what's happening to me, and sometimes everything is . . . *hazy* and hard to remember," says Kat, her big blue eyes darting to one side and the other as she struggles to explain herself. "Same as I don't understand what happened to me when I . . . when I stopped living. I just know I *have* to find out – and I can't do it on my own."

"You don't have to do it on your own," I tell Kat, covering her hand with mine. "I'll help. Of course I'll help."

"Thank you, Maisie!" she says, smiling gratefully at me. "Thank you *so* much!"

I don't know if Kat is going blurry because I'm crying now, or if she's just going blurry.

"So what's your *actual* name, Kat?" I ask, sniffing, blinking the sudden, salty tears from my eyes, keen to be properly introduced to my very special friend.

"Katherine Mary Jessop," she answers me, letting her gaze fall on the school photo that's now on my lap.

"And you were friends with Lindsey Butterfield, who lived here?"

"I *think* so," says Kat unsurely, her touch feeling lighter, her image fading in and out, like a malfunctioning projection.

I have a sudden memory of the other night, of hearing girls' laughter in Clem's empty, silent room.

One of the voices was Kat's, I now feel certain.

She knew this house.

She knew it way back in the 1980s, when Lindsey Butterfield lived here.

"Don't worry, we'll figure this out," I whisper, bending closer to her so that our two foreheads – one cold, one hot to the touch – press lightly together.

And in that still, lovely moment of wonder, I remember another page from the notebook, some words doodled in Mum's comforting handwriting: *Treasure your old friends, and be open to making new ones!*

Well, I am more freaked out than I have ever been, but – seeing as I have no old friends – I'm definitely planning on treasuring this new one, however strange she is. *Especially* if she needs my help.

"Ahem."

The "ahem" comes from a couple of metres away.

It comes from my big sister, standing on the back doorstep, staring at me.

"What?" I say sharply, heart thumping, automatically straightening up.

"Why were you hunched over like that just now, like you were constipated or something?" she calls out coolly, cattily.

I blink, and see that I'm holding hands with no one, whispering comforting words to thin air.

"None of your business," I bark back at Clem.

"Ooo-OOO-ooo! *Someone's* touchy!" my sister teases. "I only came to tell you Dad's back. He asked me to ask you if your friend wanted to stay for tea. But I guess there's no point, if she's left already."

Kat.

Katherine Mary Jessop.

Yes, she *has* left.

In some ways, she left in 1987.

But in some ways, as I've found out to my complete and utter, slap-in-the-face shock, she's never left at all. . .

13

Always remember, you're smarter than you think. Just give it time.

"Knock, knock, knock!"

Someone really is saying that, as well as doing it.

"Maisie?"

I try and drag myself out of the soft sludge of sleep and figure out where I am.

For a second I blink and wonder why the furniture is this way round, let my fingers touch the plain wallpaper and frown over where my Cath Kidson flowers have gone.

Then the pieces of my scrambled brain slot into place and I remember I'm not at 12 Park Close any more.

I'm in Nightingale Cottage.

I go to Nightingale School.

And my best friend is a ghost.

"Are you all right, honey?" Dad asks, sticking his head around the door.

Er, no, not really, I think.

Or then again, maybe I am surprisingly all right, considering.

Considering I just realized I've been hanging out with a dead person all week.

Wouldn't that blow Dad's mind? If I casually said, "Hey, you know Kat, the girl you met last Friday night? Well, she wasn't really there, if you see what I mean."

Of course he wouldn't see what I meant.

Of course he'd think I was ill.

Or going through some hugely delayed reaction to Mum dying or something, if he wanted to go all psychological on me. (Though that's more Clem's territory, since psychology is one of her A-levels. But I am definitely *not* going to tell her about this.)

"You've slept for nearly twelve hours!" Dad says with a laugh.

"Have I?" I mumble, propping myself up on my elbows and reading seven-fifty a.m. on the clock. I'll have to hurry to get myself ready for school.

"I'll stick some toast on for you, if you're hungry," he adds.

"Yeah, I'm starving."

Dad seems pleased to hear that, and disappears with a stomp, stomp, stomp down the stairs. I guess he was a bit worried I was sick or coming down with something last night, since I didn't eat any of my tea and went straight up to bed.

Of course I wasn't sick; I was just too numb and bewildered to think about food. All I'd wanted was time on my own, to sit in my room and try to make sense of the conversation I'd just had with Kat. To get it fixed in my head who she was and *what* she was. To figure out exactly how I was going to help Kat. (*Always remember,* Mum wrote in the notebook, *you're smarter than you think. Just give it time.* I wish. . .)

As I lay my head down on the pillow last night, I'd fretted over what Kat had whispered to me that first lunchtime we'd met, when she'd come up to me in the dinner hall. "I'd *love* to find out her story!" she'd said, entwining her arm in mine. I'd thought she was talking about the supposed Victorian ghost, but of course she was really talking about herself. . .

"Peanut butter? Marmite?" Dad offers as I join him in the kitchen a few minutes later, slouching on to a chair.

"Both, please," I yawn, dragging my fingers through my hair.

"What did your last servant die of, Maisie?" says Clem, breezing into the room in a hazy fug of perfume and the smell of warm hair-straightening serum. "Dad's working, remember – he's only dropped in for a second, you know!"

I can't think of a smart response; I'm too tired after my epic sleep, when my brain shut down from information overload. But then again, I can generally never think of a smart response to Clem's snippy remarks.

Luckily, I don't have to this morning; Dad leaps to my defence.

"Leave her alone, Clem; I offered," Dad tells my sister, happy to pass me my breakfast bits while he waits for the kettle to boil so he can fill his flask mug with coffee.

I expect Clem to go huffing off with a half-heard, petulant grumble, but she doesn't.

In fact, she's strangely quiet.

I glance up from the toast I'm buttering and see that my sister's eyes are narrowed, closely observing Dad as he plonks down the jars beside my plate with a cheery whistle.

"What? Have I got toast crumbs on my chin or something?" Dad asks, suddenly registering Clem's forensic gaze and brushing his face with his hands.

"*You* look very happy," she says, accusingly.

"I'm a happy sort of person! What can I tell you?" he replies, but he's grinning, as if he's in on a joke we're not part of.

"You can tell us what you're smiling about, for a start," Clem demands.

"What is it?" I join in and ask, feeling very awake now, even if I probably don't look it, with my scruffy PJs and bedhead hair.

"Well, I took my youngest daughter's advice. . ." he begins, reserving his smile for me.

"Whoa – *tell* me you didn't listen to anything *she* had to say," Clem interrupts, reserving her lazy sarcasm for me. "You *know* that's about as sensible as paddling through a piranha-infested river."

"OK, Clem, if you don't want to hear what your sister's advice was, and how it worked out, then fine," Dad says with a maddening shrug.

Maddening for Clem, since *I* know what I said. What I said when I kept Dad company as he cleaned the art room windows yesterday afternoon.

"Dad! Don't be so childish!" she accuses him, as if

she's the most grown-up of us all. Yeah, so grown-up she's looking like she might just have a tantrum if he doesn't spill his story in the next ten seconds or less.

If I wasn't so keen to find out what was going on, I'd've happily sat munching my toast, watching Dad wind her up some more. . .

"Dad – are you talking about Donna?" I ask him, feeling pretty certain it's what he means. He's taken my advice; he's asked her to be honest with him about what's going on. And he's smiling, which means it *has* to be good news, doesn't it?

"I called her up, Maisie, like you told me to," Dad acknowledges, as he pours the hot water into his flask mug.

"And what did she say?"

Out of the corner of my eye, I see Clem's gaze dart from me to Dad to me again. Not knowing what's going on must be absolutely infuriating for her.

Great!

"She apologized. She said she's sorry if she's been a bit distant; she said things had been getting on top of her."

"So it's definitely nothing to do with me and Clem?" I check.

"Wait a minute, what do you mea—"

"Definitely not," says Dad, cutting across Clem's protests. "And hey, if she had a problem with you and your sister, she wouldn't be coming here for tea with us tomorrow night, would she?"

So, *that's* what Dad's big beaming smile is all about!

"*Here?*" says Clem, her voice sounding sarky, as usual. Can't she ditch it for once? Hasn't she been hoping, same as me, that we'd meet Dad's mystery woman one day? If she keeps this up tomorrow, Donna really *might* go off the idea of us pretty quickly. . .

"Yes, here!" says Dad, screwing the lid on his flask mug. "Got a problem with that, Miss Clementine Mills?"

He's still grinning, skating over the top of Clem's negativity, which I can never manage to do (it sinks me).

"Well, *I* haven't got a problem living in this dump, surrounded by unpacked boxes, but your lovely girlfriend might."

Clem fans out her arms, looking like one of those perma-smiling models on some shopping channel, displaying the goods for sale.

Only Clem isn't smiling and what she's drawing our attention to isn't anything anyone would want to pay money for.

I hate to say it, but she's right.

Apart from a few favourite things propped on the shelves, the rest of the kitchen still looks like we moved in twenty minutes ago.

"It's only been a week and a half, and you've had your new job to concentrate on," I say to Dad, seeing him wince at the clutter we've been too busy living with to notice.

But Dad doesn't seem to register my comforting words, and begins rubbing his face with his hands.

"Maybe I should book us into a restaurant," he mumbles.

"No, you *won't*," says Clem.

"What's going on with you?" I find myself snapping at her. "One minute you're making out this place is too scuzzy to bring Donna back to, then the next, you're telling Dad he *shouldn't* cancel."

"Look, if Donna is coming, it's serious. I mean they're serious; in a good way, right?" she says, talking to me as if I have the brain of a small, dim slug.

"Right," I reply.

I notice that now it's Dad's turn to stare from one to the other of us, confused.

"So Donna needs to meet us. She needs to see the hovel," says Clem, doing her shopping-channel-hostess act again and fanning her arms out. "If she still likes Dad after she's seen this place and we've grilled her—"

"Clem!" Dad gasps in alarm.

"Joking!" she sighs, rolling her eyes. "*As* I was saying, if Donna can handle the sight of me and Maisie *and* our dismal home, then she is bound to be a good person."

"Er . . . OK," Dad says dubiously, staring at Clem, then staring at the teetering mountain of brown boxes cluttering up one side of the kitchen.

"And me and Maisie will help you blitz this place tonight. Right, Maisie?"

"Right," I say again, as if I'm answering a sergeant major.

But if it helps Dad and Donna be happy, I'm happy – just this once – to be ordered about.

"What can I say? Thanks, girls; that's great," Dad laughs happily, stunned at Clem's kind offer. "Well, till tonight, then. I better go and shoo away parents trying to park outside the entrance, as usual. . ."

"Not so fast," says Clem, putting an arm out to stop him passing. "What are you making for tea?"

"Oh! I, uh, I'm not really sure. . ."

"Your Italian stuff's really nice. Do that," says Clem, sounding like a bossy head chef now. "And there's that new deli in town – they do real sun-dried tomatoes and posh fresh pesto and everything. Write a list and leave it for us. Maisie will go after school."

"Will I?" I say, startled at the rate these orders are coming.

"Well, *duh*!" says Clem. "*I* can't go 'cause I'm dip-dying the ends of Bea's hair blue, aren't I?"

There's no arguing with that, I guess.

And I don't have the energy to argue with Clem anyway, not when I'm more concerned with problems I've got to solve, like how exactly I can help Kat. I mean, where do I begin?

"*What* new deli?" Dad asks Clem, at the same time as checking his watch and knowing he needs to get a move on.

"It's right by that café that opened a couple of years ago. The one with all the vintage plates and cups and cake stands in the window. What's it called again?"

I frown. I think. I *do* know it; Lilah's mum took

her, me and Jasneet there when it first opened. We had scones and jam and cream and all felt wonderfully full and slightly sick after.

Oh, *why* can't I remember?

Maybe it's because my mind is too fixated on finding clues to unlock Kat's story.

Not that I'm likely to stumble on one here, in our messy kitchen, surrounded by boxes and clutter and breakfast plates.

"Oh!" gasps Clem, suddenly looking like she's been slapped around the face. "I remember now; the name of the café . . . it's *Butterfield's*!"

"No way!" Dad says with a grin. "The name of the old site manager of the school? That's a bit of a coincidence, isn't it?"

I'd say it's *much* more than a bit of a coincidence.

Mum's advice is right; I just needed to give my smartness some time. 'Cause it occurs to me that the first piece of Katherine Mary Jessop's puzzle has something to do with the box we – *she* – found in the summerhouse. And now I have a fuzzy but somehow sure feeling that the second piece of the puzzle has just dropped into place, and I can't wait to tell Kat all about it. . .

*

Buddhists have mantras.

And anyone who's into meditating has mantras too, words or phrases they repeat over and over again.

I'm repeating my own mantra now.

"Where are you, Kat? Where are you, Kat? Where are you, Kat?" in a voice so low that no one can hear, though they may see my lips moving, I guess. (Patience gave me a quizzical look in maths class, but thankfully she didn't nudge anyone else so they could gawp at me too.)

I'm desperate to see Kat, but I'm desperately worried too. The more she appears, the more exhausted she gets. Was helping me through the shock yesterday too much for her? I haven't seen her anywhere so far today. The corridors buzz with girls who aren't Kat, the packed dinner hall felt empty without her at lunch, the sprawling green lawn with its blossom-laden trees seems a khaki shade of grey without the presence of my best friend.

"Where are you, Kat? Where are you, Kat? Where are you, Kat?" I mumble almost silently as I let myself be bustled along the first-floor corridor, past the art room on the way to French.

And then I spot something out of the corner of my eye.

A shift.

A stutter of a movement that doesn't match the bustle and amble of students going on around me.

It's like a now-you-see-it, now-you-don't image.

A girl with huge blue eyes and a floppy hair bow.

"Sorry – oops! My fault. Sorry," I say, turning against the tide and making my way over to Kat. She's leaning against the wall of the art room, her head resting on the frosted glass panels that run the length of it.

"Where've you been?" I ask her.

"Just the usual – nowhere-land," says Kat, giving me one of her wry, apologetic smiles. "Getting my energy back, I guess."

"Well, I'm glad you're here now, 'cause I've found out something. . ."

With that, I rifle in my bag, pulling out the shortbread tin from the summerhouse.

"Look," I say, popping it open and pulling out the class photo of Kat and her classmates. "This – this is Lindsey Butterfield, right?"

"Mmm," mutters Kat, nodding.

"Well, I know who she is!" I announce.

"The old site manager's daughter," says Kat. "She

used to live in your house. She was maybe my friend."

Kat's just repeating what we've already figured out.

She doesn't know that I know *more*.

"I've seen her, Kat! Grown up, I mean. She runs a café in town."

It came back to me in the shower, when I gave myself a bit of thinking time (just like Mum said). I remembered this cheery, slightly plump blonde woman who served us the time we went in with Lilah's mother. The café was newly opened back then, and Lilah's mum spent ages talking to the friendly owner about how it was going. The friendly owner who I *absolutely* recognized from the 1987 photo as being an older version of Lindsey, even if the Butterfield's name hadn't been a ginormous giveaway.

"Is that good?" asks Kat, trying hard to understand my excitement.

"Maybe!" I say hurriedly, noticing that the crowds are thinning out, that I'm going to be late for class if I'm not careful. "I think we need to go and see Lindsey . . . she's *got* to be able to tell us about your –"

I stumble, only just avoiding using the word "death". It's such a harsh, heavy word.

"– of what happened to you, I mean," I quickly correct myself.

"Maisie? What are you doing here? Shouldn't you be in class now?" a friendly but teacherly voice suddenly asks. It's Miss Carrera, swooping out of the art room in one of her long white aprons. The hem of it brushes Kat's leg, but she seems unaware. I guess it's just me who can see Kat right now.

"I'm going, I'm going," I assure Miss Carrera.

Then I notice Kat waver like some mirage, a hovering, vibrating image of my friend. She's there and then she's not, in split-second rotations.

"Maisie? What's wrong?" I hear Miss Carrera's voice ask, full of concern. "Why are you staring at the wall?"

But I'm not staring at the wall – I'm looking at my friend, wondering what's happening to her, what's wrong with her.

She's sinking down, down, fainting away.

"No!" I call out, crouching to catch her, to cradle her in my arms.

Her eyes are fluttering, as if she's slipping into unconsciousness. . .

And then she's gone.

"Maisie! *Maisie!*" I vaguely hear Miss Carrera say, only half-aware of her arms around my shoulders.

And here I am, crouching on the ground.

As far as Miss Carrera and any last-minute, late-running students can see, I'm holding nothing but thin air. . .

14 It's always nice to be nice!

"The bottom line is, I'm worried about you."

I don't look at Mrs Watson – I just stare down at the selection of biscuits she's placed on a rose-patterned plate in front of me. I haven't touched one.

"Please don't be," I say, shuffling on her squelchy leatherette visitors' chair.

"Well, I am. Students don't go crumpling to the floor in corridors for no reason."

She's saying it kindly, with a bit of humour in her voice, hoping I'll respond with a smile, open up to her.

But it's not going to happen.

I have to protect myself – and Kat.

"I felt a bit dizzy for a second, that's all."

"Yes, but is it because you haven't eaten enough today?"

"I had lunch."

"Which was. . .?"

"Macaroni cheese," I tell her.

I don't tell her I ate about a mouthful of it and it tasted like boiled rubber tubing. No offence to the school cooks, but when you're consumed with finding your fading dead friend, you *kind* of lose your appetite.

"Dehydration, then. What have you drunk so far today?"

"Orange juice at breakfast time, squash at lunch, and here –" I take a practically empty water bottle from my bag "– I've had most of this."

"Well, it's something else, then. Having you been feeling unwell recently, Maisie?"

"No, Mrs Watson," I say, both to her question and the plate of biscuits she's waggling under my nose.

With everything that's happening at the moment, I've been feeling the opposite of unwell. I'm brimming full of spangles and excitement and wonder.

"Been feeling headachey? Migraines? Is it that time of the month? Are you feverish?" she tries, giving up on the biscuits and plopping them back down on her table.

When Miss Carrera phoned down to the office, and Mahalia and her first-aid skills rushed to my rescue, I thought that was it. I didn't expect to get this cheery but determined grilling from my form teacher.

"No, Mrs Watson."

"You know, it *might* be that you're anaemic . . . lacking in iron, that is. It's quite common in your early teens. Tell you what, I'll mention to your dad that he should take you to your doctor – have you tested."

It's on the tip of my tongue to jump in and tell her no, *please* don't mention anything to Dad, but if I panic and get flustered it'll look bad, as if I'm hiding something (a ghost, actually).

Luckily a sentence flashes into my head – fluttering from the well-worn pages of Mum's notebook – which shows me how I have to play this.

"Actually, I have to go for a check-up next week, for an . . . ear thing I have," I say nicely (*It's always nice to be nice*). "I could ask the doctor about the anaemia thing then?"

Yes, I am saying this nicely.

Yes, I am also lying.

But it *is* getting Mrs Watson off my back for now, I hope, and stopping her from involving Dad.

"Good! Good thinking, Maisie," she replies positively. "And ear problems often cause balance issues, you know, so do tell your doctor about what happened in the art room corridor just now."

"I will," I say.

I won't, I think.

"Good, good," says Mrs Watson, with an approving nod.

Can I go now, can I go now, can I go now, I mutter silently to myself, putting my hands on the armrests of the chair, hoping I can say thank you (nicely) and get back to class.

"And there's nothing at all troubling you, is there, Maisie?"

Ah, it's not over yet.

"No, Mrs Watson."

"Nothing's making you unhappy?"

It's the opposite. I haven't felt so happy in a long time.

"The girls here are being nice to you? You're making friends?"

"Yes, miss."

The girls here are steering clear of me, but I don't care, 'cause I *do* have a friend. The most special, amazing, out-of-this-world friend. Who I really need to find and check that she's all right. . .

"It's just that you do seem to be on your own rather a lot. Miss Carrera *and* Mrs Gupta in the library mentioned it, and the office staff have noticed too. . ."

For their information, I'm not on my own. But I'm not about to say that, of course.

"I sometimes like to be by myself," I answer as pleasantly as possible.

"Hmm. You know, I'm hoping you haven't got some, say . . . deep, dark secret on your mind, Maisie," says Mrs Watson, her eyes boring into mine, as if she's trying to see what's going on inside my head.

Well, I *do* happen to have a secret in there, of course, but it's not deep or dark; it's shiny and amazing. And there's no way I'm going to let Mrs Watson know about it, so I drop my eyes to the plate of biscuits.

"Honestly, I'm fine. Can I have one of those after all?"

"Yes, yes! *Please* do. Take two," Mrs Watson says enthusiastically, taking this sudden interest in snacks as a sure sign of returning good health and spirits, just as I hoped.

I nibble my way through the first one (though it's like eating crunchy cardboard coated in chocolate) and shuffle slightly, readying myself for goodbyes.

"The thing is, Maisie, without raking up the past, you obviously know that I have your records from your last school and I *am* aware of the . . . the *incident* that happened there."

Oh.

That.

All the spangles and excitement and wonder fade away from me and I'm plunged into a moment of gloom.

"Right, so it *is* that. I see."

Mrs Watson – spotting my expression – thinks she found the source of my woes, the reason for my crumple in the corridor.

I say nothing.

"But I want you to know something, Maisie," Mrs Watson carries on, craning forward in her seat so she can be more in-my-face earnest. "Coming here to Nightingale School, it's a new start, a clean slate."

"I didn't hurt the other girl deliberately, Mrs Watson – I really didn't," I say hurriedly, hating this unexpected wave of old pain. "But no one believed me!"

"Maisie, your father talked me through what happened," she surprises me by saying. "And although it's probably unprofessional of me to say so, I think the situation wasn't handled very well by the head at Park View. . ."

Mrs Watson doesn't go so far as to say she sides with me, but the way her voice trails off, I know she does. And that suddenly feels so, *so* good.

"Look, Maisie, the bottom line is, no one here knows about the accident – apart from me, of course. Do you understand?"

Actually, it might not be just you, Mrs Watson, I think, the good feeling slipping slightly as I picture the wary sideways glances I've been getting from Hannah and Natasha and Patience and the others.

Still, it's Kat who's helped me the most so far, and I have to remind myself that she's who and what matters most right now. I'm not going to let thoughts of Saffy Price and her lies linger any more. . .

"Thank you, Mrs Watson. May I go now?" I say just as nicely as I can as I get up from my chair.

"Um, of course," she replies, slightly startled by my forthrightness. "But remember, my door is always open if you need to chat. . ."

As I leave, I realize – with shock – that I owe

someone *very* unexpected a great big thank you.

Because if Mrs Watson thinks anything of my behaviour is odd, from now on she'll put it down to me having a wobble about "the incident".

So thanks, Saffy, my worst enemy, for getting my form teacher off my back, and letting me get on with my new life with my strange and special new friend. . .

15

You're always braver than you think you are..

"Is this OK?" asks Kat, sitting perched on the stool in front of Clem's dressing table.

Her hands are in her lap, her fingers fidgeting with the soft, silky navy bow I made her untie from around her head.

"No. It's highly, *highly* dangerous," I tell Kat.

I'm not talking about the straighteners I'm using, trying to tame her big, wavy hair right now.

I'm talking about being here in Clem's room. If my sister knew, she'd kill us both (though I guess that wouldn't matter too much in Kat's case).

But Clem isn't due back from her college across town for another twenty minutes at least. Which is all the time I need.

"We should be quick, then?" Kat blinks at me in the mirror.

"We'll be quick," I assure her.

We'll be quick for two reasons: first, Butterfield's café shuts fairly soon, once the afternoon tea and cake customers wander home. I know this from my trip to the new deli yesterday – when I peeked next door at the café, my heart thundering as I spotted the grown-up Lindsey sweeping the floor inside.

Secondly, I know Kat has limited energy. After yesterday's fade-away in the art room corridor, it's taken her till now, after school on Wednesday, to properly reappear to me.

To be honest, I don't know how she'll have the strength to stay in plain view this afternoon. Maybe I should check that Kat's totally sure about this. . .

"Remember, you don't *have* to show yourself," I pause and tell her reflection. "I can just go into the café on my own – with you beside me, but not visible to Lindsey. It'd be a lot less tiring for you that way."

"But I was *once* real to her, and I'd like to feel like a real girl next to her, just one more time," Kat says very certainly. "Maybe it'll help me remember more."

"Even though you'll be in disguise?" I remind her. We don't want to risk shocking Lindsey Butterfield so much that she faints clean away and can tell us nothing.

"Yes, even though I'll be in disguise. Even though I look *weird*," Kat says, pulling an unimpressed face as her hair is smoothed out, section by section. "Doesn't it look . . . lanky?"

She holds up a straightened section of her fair hair and lets it drop, *plop*.

"No – it's gorgeous," I tell her. "I know it's not your style, but it'll mean you'll fit right in, I promise."

"Well, if you say so," says Kat dubiously. But dubious or not, I know she's putting her trust in me, and that's a pretty lovely feeling, actually.

"Now for the make-up. . ." I say, finishing my last lap with the straighteners and studying Clem's impressive array of beauty products spread out in front of the dressing table mirror.

I reach for the make-up remover and cotton pads first.

"Close your eyes," I tell my friend as I start swooping the dampened pad over her eyes, to take off the thick mascara.

It doesn't budge.

I check the cotton pad; it doesn't have a mark on it.

Confused, I try dabbing at the pinky-bronze blusher on Kat's cheeks . . . same result, i.e., *no* result.

It seems that ghosts just look the way they look. Kat's eighties make-up is part of her. There isn't a cleansing lotion invented that's going to make it vanish.

"Is something wrong?" Kat asks, aware of my sudden silence.

"Nothing's wrong, I'm just going to try something else," I bluster, not wanting to make Kat feel unsure of herself; it might sap whatever energy she has today. "Let's try this. . ."

Yes. Thank goodness. I can at least put make-up *on* to Kat. And Clem's warm-toned, natural foundation gives Kat a healthier glow than she's had lately, cancelling out her pale skin, the dark rings under her eyes, the obvious, old-fashioned blast of blusher.

Then last it's a slick of light rosy-brown lip salve to cover up the pale, glittery-pink gloss she's so fond of.

"There," I say, standing back and letting Kat spin around to check out her transformation into a twenty-first century girl.

"Wow," she says uncertainly. "I really *am* in disguise. . ."

"Yep," I agree with her, not taking it personally. Flipping it around the other way, I don't suppose

I'd be a hundred per cent thrilled if someone made *me* over as a puff-haired, over-made-up eighties girl. "There's no way Lindsey will recognize you!"

"I don't recognize *myself*," says Kat, turning this way and that. "Don't I need some colour on my cheeks at least?"

"*No*," I say firmly. "But hey, I've thought of one more thing. . ."

I run through to my room, rummage in the last box I've still to unpack – one with all the random stuff I ran out of energy to sort neatly – and pretty quickly find what I'm looking for.

"Don't laugh," I say, hurrying back to Kat and presenting her with some thick black-rimmed specs I bought a couple of summers ago from H&M along with this cute T-shirt with "GEEK" written on it in big letters. "They've only got plain glass in them. Well, plastic."

"Aw, cute!" she says, immediately putting them on. "Morrissey wears ones just like these!"

I'm about to ask who Morrissey is, then vaguely remember that he's a singer Dad used to like when he was at uni, from a band called the Stranglers, I think. Or was it the Smiths?

But there's no time for musing over Dad's old

vinyl collection; spotting the reflection of Clem's bedside clock in the mirror, I realize Kat and I really need to move it and get to the café before its owner locks up for the day and heads home.

Gulp.

Just what is middle-aged Lindsey Butterfield going to make of girls in Nightingale School uniforms turning up at her work clutching a shortbread tin. . .?

"All right?" I check with Kat.

"No," says the girl next to me, who doesn't look very much like the Kat I know, which is good, in the circumstances.

The circumstances being, we're standing on the pavement across the road from Butterfield's café, watching a blissfully ignorant Lindsey Butterfield turning the *Open* sign to *Closed*.

It's OK, there's still time; she starts cleaning up now. I watched her do it yesterday, as I hovered with my jar of pesto, posh pasta and other stuff Dad had asked me to pick up from the deli next door.

"No?" I repeat anxiously, then turn to see that Kat is nervously smiling, so I know she's just messing with me. Sort of.

"So, are you ready?" I check with her, taking a deep breath myself and reaching out to her with my left hand (the shortbread tin is in my right, clutched to my chest).

"No," she half-jokes again, taking my hand and letting me pull her across the road, through a gap in the traffic.

We hesitate again, just outside the café.

"We're braver than we think, OK?" I say to Kat, pretending I'm reassuring her, though I'm really reassuring myself. (I'm paraphrasing one of my mum's notes-to-me-and-Clem. I have never felt *less* brave. At least not since last Monday, five minutes before I had to walk into my new school.)

"OK," says Kat, her blue eyes blinking trustingly at me through the plastic lenses of her chunky black glasses. "Then let's do it. . ."

My voice has a helium squeak to it; my hand is shaking as I tap on the glass.

"Sorry! We're closed!" the blonde woman – Lindsey – mouths at us as she stacks chairs on tables, ready to mop the floor.

I try beckoning her.

She gives a rueful, sorry smile and shake of her head, and points to her watch.

Help. She thinks we're after a last-minute latte and a chunk of carrot cake. Not information that might solve the mystery of a long-dead schoolmate. Who's, er, standing right beside me.

"The tin!" says Kat. "Hold the tin up!"

It's a good idea, so I do it.

I turn the front of the tin towards Lindsey, hoping she can see the Scottie and the Westie nuzzled up together. Hoping those dogs and the twee tartan trim of the tin box will bring some long-forgotten memory flipping to the forefront of her mind.

Yes! I think it might be working.

Lindsey frowns.

Walks a little closer.

Tucks a lock of her now-dyed-blonde hair behind her ear as she concentrates.

Then her eyes suddenly widen, her brows arching high in surprise.

Bingo. . .

The door is pulled open with a tinkle of a bell, and we find ourselves being ushered inside.

Pow – we're immediately hit by the rich scents of sweetness and coffee grounds. The smell mingles with the sounds of some man in a clipped English voice crooning over a jaunty ragtime piano.

"Let me turn the music down," says Lindsey, bustling over to an iPod dock set behind the retro wooden counter.

I shoot a sideways glance at Kat, who's tilting her head to one side, deliberately letting a curtain of hair drape over her face, helping to hide it. (Guess she's still not totally secure in the disguise of her new-look appearance.)

"Please, have a seat," says Lindsey, walking back towards us and ushering us to sit at one of the tables where the chairs haven't been stacked on top yet.

"Thanks," I say shyly, perching on the edge of the chair nearest to me.

Kat seems to hesitate, letting Lindsey choose her seat first – then she sits down right next to her.

I'm sort of surprised, thinking my friend would've been so nervous she would be practically velcro'd to my side. Then in a split second, I figure out *why* she's done it: Lindsey won't get such a good view of Kat side on. And sure enough, the café owner is looking directly at me now.

"Is this what I think it is?" she says with a hopeful smile, the fingers of her veined hands tapping lightly on the tin box.

"My name's Maisie, and me and my friend. . ." I begin – then stumble over how to introduce Kat.

"Patience," Kat jumps in, perhaps just grabbing hold of the first girl's name that popped into her head.

"Yeah, me and my friend Patience found it," I carry on. "I live in Nightingale Cottage now; my dad is the new site manager."

"Really? My old house!" Lindsey beams. "My father was the site manager there until a few months ago. Of course, I remember the days when he was called caretaker, and before that, janitor. . ."

Lindsey's face softens, her head swirling with memories of her childhood, I guess.

"I hoped this was yours, when I remembered the name of this café. . ." I say, nodding at the tin.

"Yes, I suppose it's useful that it's an unusual name!" Lindsey admits. "But where did you find this? I was there helping Dad pack up before he moved to his retirement flat. I thought we'd got everything."

"It was hidden under the seat in the old summerhouse," I tell her.

"Of *course*!" says Lindsey, rolling her eyes. "I moved it out there when my brother Gary raided my room once. I hated him looking through my stuff. He'd do it just to bug me. You know what little brothers are like!"

I smile, though I don't know, of course, only having a fearsome big sister myself. And Kat; she has – *had* – a little sister. I've never found out any more about her, or Kat's mum.

Actually, what did Kat say the other day when she didn't want to go home? "I'm not my mum's favourite person right now. . ." I should ask her about that. Though she might not have an answer anyway. Lots of information seems to come to Kat in wisps of half-remembered moments.

"I've forgotten what I put in here," Lindsey continues, pulling the tin towards her and scrabbling to open the tight, slightly rusty lid with her nails. "And to be honest, I thought Dad must've thrown it out. Just before he moved he had a clear-out of lots of my and Gary's old stuff from our schooldays. Some of it went in the bin, some of it he donated to the art teacher, for the kids' projects, he told us. Wow, this is wedged tight!"

"Here, let me," says Kat, taking the tin from her and using her slim, white-knuckled fingers to prise the lid open. I hope she doesn't use up too much energy doing such a human task, but she's so desperate to see if Lindsey has some answers for her that I suppose she's willing to risk it.

"I was so cross with Dad for doing that without checking with me and Gary first," Lindsey chatters on, "but as he said, 'Well, if you two were so keen on that old rubbish you'd've come and collected it years ago.' He had a point, I suppose."

"What sort of stuff was it?" I ask, imagining how awful it would be if Dad threw out some of my special things, like all the notebooks I doodle in – even *Mum's notebook*, by accident – and shudder.

"Oh, I had a pile of my favourite *Just Seventeen* and *Smash Hits* magazines," Lindsey reminisces as Kat's fingernails scrabble on metal, trying to get a grip. "And all my old tapes! Me and my friends loved hanging out in my room, listening to music. . ."

As Lindsey's gaze drifts off, remembering herself in what's now Clem's room (mine must've been Gary's?), I notice that Kat has frozen; has something Lindsey's said set free a flicker of some long-lost image for her?

Before Lindsey spots her sudden stillness, I reach over and grab the tin from my friend. Her eyes – framed in black – are wide and staring, as if focused in concentration as her mind jumps around, trying to catch hold of the fluttering butterfly of the memory.

"Give's a go," I say brightly, while Lindsey happily rambles on.

"You know, I was the first in my class to get a Walkman – one of those portable machines that played tapes, I mean. You girls won't remember *those*."

I politely shake my head, though I think Dad *has* mentioned them, when I've not really been listening too closely (sorry, Dad).

"Then when I was at uni, I got myself a CD Walkman too," Lindsey carries on, "and bought my favourite music all over again! So yes, the tapes, the CDs, the Walkmans, the magazines . . . all gone."

Clang!

The tin lid finally gives, goes clattering across the pretty rose-speckled tablecloth and hits the sugar bowl.

"Whoops!" laughs Lindsey, catching it. "Well, let's see what's in here, shall we?"

She begins to take out the contents of the tin, studying it bit by bit, laying it out over the roses.

"I *loved* these hair combs. . . I used to wear my

hair up a lot. Oh, look at this – postcards from Jenny and Susan and Helen! I used to be so jealous that they went abroad for their holidays. My family always went to rainy caravan parks in Wales, or up to the Lake District if we were lucky. . ."

Lindsey chats away, full of wonder at every scrap, every badge, every cinema ticket stub, every piece of paraphernalia.

I look and smile and ask interested questions now and then, sneaking the odd peek at Kat, who still seems vague and unsettled, and nibbling her nails.

"And this! This I must have torn from a copy of *Smash Hits*," says Lindsey, holding up the Top Ten Singles list I remember coming across in the summerhouse with Kat. "It's from 1987. I was crazy about almost every track on there. Especially 'La Bamba'! It was from the soundtrack of a film we were all mad about."

"La Bamba"?! The song Kat sang the evening we snuck around school. . . The track on the CD that Miss Carrera played yesterday. . .

She cut it off the junk sculpture, I remind myself.

Was that CD part of Lindsey's recently junked stash? The stuff old Mr Butterfield cleared out before she or her brother could stop him. . .?

Kat is biting her lip, shooting me a small, secret smile.

She knows what I'm thinking and she's letting me know I'm right: we've just stumbled on the third piece of the puzzle.

"You know, I was *so* totally in love with the lead actor, Lou Diamond Phillips," Lindsey says with a wistful laugh, unaware of the looks me and Kat have just exchanged. "Well, we *all* were! And actually, I remember this one time a girl in my class came around to mine and we even made up our own dance to the song. How funny is that?"

Very funny, think. I heard the traces of your forgotten laughter the other night.

"Katherine; *that* was her name. . ."

Katherine slides slightly down in her seat next to Lindsey, through shock at hearing her name or an attempt to hide herself away, I don't know.

She's blinking at me behind the curtains of her straightened hair.

But at the mention of Kat's name, Lindsey's smile fades, and she falls silent.

"Was Katherine your best friend?" I say.

It's not the question I really want to ask, but if I rush in with, "So what happened to Katherine?"

then Lindsey will know we know more than we're letting on.

"No . . . I mean, I liked her, but Helen Smith was my best friend. *Katherine* was just part of the extended gang. We all played netball in the same team."

Lindsey must have pictures flashing in her head right now, which means the truth about Kat is *in* there, though I don't suppose she's suddenly going to blurt it out to two impressionable thirteen-year-olds she's never met before.

What she knows is upsetting, you can tell from her face. But it's *exactly* the sort of information that we want to know.

How do I ease her into telling us?

Then I have an idea.

"My – I mean, *our* – art teacher told us that she heard that something very sad happened to your dad once," I say, then leave the statement hanging in the air.

"Ah, yes. . ." Lindsey replies thoughtfully, at the same time lifting out the last item left in the tin box – the class photo.

I hold my breath.

I wonder if Kat's doing the same thing, and then

remember that breathing isn't something she needs to do.

"There was some kind of accident after school one day," Lindsey says, studying her old schoolmate's circled face in the picture. "Katherine died. My dad was the first one to find her. He tried to help her, to save her, but she was gone. It absolutely wrecked him. He was off work with depression for quite a while afterwards."

So *that's* what happened to Mr Butterfield. It's good to clear up the mystery surrounding him – but the expression on Lindsey's face is so sad that I almost feel guilty for forcing these memories on her. . .

"What happened? What sort of accident was it?" I press on, feeling like we're so close to finding the fourth and fattest clue to the puzzle of Kat's life – and death – so far.

"I don't know; none of us did," Lindsey glances up at me, gives me a rueful smile. "It was different back then; no one liked to talk about bad stuff. Nowadays, there'd be a memorial assembly, offers of counsellors for Dad and for her classmates."

"I guess so," I say in a small voice, disappointed

that the story seems to be grinding to a halt here. "But didn't your dad tell you and your family *anything*?"

"No – the subject was closed to my brother and me, even though she was in my class. When I asked my mum about it, she just said Dad had been so affected by Katherine's death that he never wanted to talk about it."

"Might he talk about it now? Now that he's not living at the school?"

"He's got some heart problems now; I wouldn't want to upset him in any way," says Lindsey, looking a little sad and concerned, which stops me in my tracks, of course.

But I'm distracted by unexpected movement.

It's Kat, holding up her right hand – the one further away from Lindsey's line of vision – and giving me one of those little-kid waves she does.

Only this time I'm not laughing, 'cause Kat is doing it to flag up the fact that she's in trouble.

Her hand may be waving, but her whole body is beginning, ever so slightly, to *waver*. Faintness is coming in ripples, as her energy fades.

I *have* to get her out of here.

"Sorry – just realized the time!" I announce,

looking down at my wrist and hoping Lindsey doesn't notice that I'm not wearing a watch. "My dad's expecting me; we have to go."

"Oh . . . oh, sure. Well, thank you for bringing me this!" says Lindsey as we screech our chairs back and I let Kat go in front of me, so I can semi-hide what's happening to her.

(It's as if sheets of tracing paper are unrolling between us, making Kat's colours and outline grainier with every unfurl.)

"That's OK!" I say cheerily, over my shoulder.

The shop bell tring-a-lings; at least Kat has had the strength to a) keep herself visible to Lindsey for as long as possible, and b) open the door. I take it from her, still directing my nothing's-wrong-nothing's-weird smile at Lindsey.

"Come again, girls, won't you?" she calls out to us. "Coffee and cake on the house next time. Your reward for finding the tin!"

"We'll definitely do that!" I lie, knowing Kat won't risk this exhausting trip away from school again.

I don't know *how* I'm going to get her home without her being seen in the most frightening of ways to passers-by. If one second she's there, next she's not, someone will end up snapping her on their mobile phone and the photos will be on tonight's *news*.

With a shaking hand I pull the door closed and then turn to see what sort of shape Kat is in.

"Maisie?"

The man's voice is warm and friendly, *same* as he is.

"Dad?" I say, panicking.

What's he doing here, *now*? When me and Kat are in this mess?

"Just been to the deli – forgot to ask you to get that nice Serrano ham yesterday. But why are you here? Are you on your own?" Dad glances around hopefully for signs of new friends.

He'll be disappointed.

But I am relieved.

There is no one else on the pavement except me and Dad.

Kat's gone, as if she never, ever existed. . .

Smile – it could brighten your day, and someone else's too.

"How do I look?" I ask Mum.

The thirteen-year-old version of her grins at me encouragingly from the youth-club-disco photo propped up on my chest of drawers.

She seems to approve. Do I?

I take a step sideways and check myself out in the full-length mirror on the inside of my wardrobe door.

A long grey T-shirt with a sketchy, distressed print of New York on it, black leggings, black pumps. It looks casual but not scruffy. Like I care, but I'm not trying *too* hard. What will Donna be wearing, I wonder?

But hey, now I think about it, maybe I just need one extra touch. . .

I go back to the dressing table.

"What do you think?" I ask Mum again. "This –"

I hold up a cute daisy hair clip to the side of my head.

"– or this?"

It's a jewelled one this time, but neither of them feels quite right for meeting Donna. The cute daisy clip suddenly seems a bit little-girly, the glitzy jewelled one too fancy.

"*I* know," I mumble, rifling in one of my drawers for a thin chiffon scarf I think is balled up in there. It's black with cream polka dots; Clem got it for my last birthday.

Now, if I just tie it around my head instead of wrapping it around my neck, it could look pretty good.

Back to the mirror. . .

Oh.

It's like I've channelled Kat's style. The floppy soft bow falls to the left side of my long, straight hair. But the look doesn't work without big, backcombed eighties waves to go with it, and I quickly yank the flimsy material off my head.

And then a prickle of panic flutters in my chest: where's Kat's navy scarf? We took it off when I straightened her hair yesterday after school. Is it still draped over Clem's dressing table? Can't be; I'd have heard my sister's Three Bears growl of "Who's been in my room?" by now.

Oh, *I* remember; just before we left, Kat scrunched it up and slipped it into her blazer pocket.

But really, the scarf isn't the important thing. Where is *she*?

I couldn't sleep last night for worrying about her. I mean, what if Kat wears her energy out completely so that one of these days she just vanishes altogether? Maybe yesterday was too much for her. Coming here, having the makeover, going into town to visit Lindsey Butterfield in the café.

By transforming her, encouraging her, have I made a huge mistake? I mean, I basically forced Kat to come *way* out of her comfort zone, didn't I?

And she wasn't at school today.

She might *never* be back at school again, and if that's the case then it'll be all my fault . . . and what would I do without her?

"Girls!" Dad calls up, shaking me out of my muddle of troubled thoughts. "Donna's here!"

"Coming!" I call back, hurrying out on to the upstairs landing at exactly the same time as Clem bursts out of her room.

Her hair is immaculately straightened, her skinny jeans tight, her baggy coral jumper slipping casually off one shoulder.

But her expression is far from casual.

In fact, it's an expression I've never seen on Clem's face for as long as I can remember.

"Are you *nervous*?" I whisper to her, which is a stupid thing to ask, 'cause it immediately gets Clem on the defensive.

"No! If anyone's going to be nervous around here, it's going to be *her*!"

Oops – Clem said that a little too loudly. Probably because she's nervous, and not about to admit it.

The problem is that my sister's bedroom door is at the top of the stairs – and standing at the bottom is our shell-shocked dad and a shyly smiling woman with red wavy hair swept into a messy, loose bun.

"Clem!" Dad starts, shocked and embarrassed.

"No – it's fine, Jack," says the red-haired woman. "Your daughter's absolutely right. I have to admit I'm a little bit shaky, meeting everyone, being here. . ."

I'm frozen to the spot, not sure what to do. I've accidentally caused the most awkward introduction ever. Dad's wincing, Donna probably wishes she could turn and leave and Clem is no doubt seething, and would storm back in her room and slam the door in my face if we didn't have a VIP in the house right now.

"Sorry," says Clem, suddenly sparking to life and sallying down the stairs, with me stumbling and bumbling down beside her like four-day-old foal. "I just meant that I don't envy you, knowing you've got to come here tonight and wondering how you're going to get on with us!"

Clem's tone is now confident and clever, and she's holding out her hand to shake Donna's in a very mature manner.

But it's only when I take a sideways peek at my sister that I realize she's forgotten to smile, which is making Donna's *own* fledgling smile falter.

A fleeting glance at Dad tells me he's struggling, not sure if Clem is being friendly or feisty, not sure how to make everything OK for the four of us.

And then, as I hover uselessly on the last step of the stairs, it comes to me. (*Smile – it could brighten your day, and someone else's too.* Thank you, Mum, for that one particular notebook tip – it drifted into my head at just the right time.)

So I smile.

Donna looks at me over Clem's shoulder and her face relaxes into a smile to match mine.

It's infectious.

Dad glances from one of us to the other and a grin breaks out.

"This is Maisie," he says proudly, "and you've already met Clem."

"Yes, I certainly have," Donna laughs, and I like the dimples that appear in the middle of her cheeks.

The bubble of tension is most definitely burst.

"Right, then!" says Dad, sounding happy and relieved. "Come on through to the kitchen, and I'll make us all a cup of tea."

"Are you kidding, Dad? I think Donna could do with a glass of that wine you've bought specially," says Clem, stalking over to the fridge and taking over as the drinks waiter while Dad and Donna exchange looks and giggle.

"Well, I don't mind if I do," says Donna, still a little uncertain as to where to stand and what to do with her purple leather handbag. She tugs her matching purple cardie over her grey, silky shift dress.

"Here," I say, hastily pulling out a chair.

"Thank you," she replies, taking up my offer and sitting at the table, which now has a bunch of bright flowers on it, bright enough to match the patterns on the Spanish vase I took down from the kitchen shelf earlier.

"Oi, Maisie – glasses!" Clem orders me as she wrestles the cork off the wine bottle, stepping away from Dad's helping hands.

I normally hate my sister bossing me about, but right now I'm happy to be given a task to do.

"Well, looks like I'm practically redundant in my own home!" I hear Dad joke as I go to open the nearest cupboard, then shut it quickly again before Donna can see the teetering piles of mess stashed in there, unpacked hurriedly from the last of the cardboard boxes that had been stacked on the kitchen floor till about fifteen minutes ago.

With a quick thwack of several more doors, I manage to locate two mismatched stemmed glasses, and figure I'll try to pass the one with the tiny chip in the rim to Dad as soon as Clem pours the wine.

As I set them down on the table, I see Dad is busying himself slooshing orange juice out for me and Clem.

Liquid glugs from bottle and carton, tinkling

glasses are passed, and Dad is suddenly sheepish again.

"Cheers!" Clem calls out loudly into the vacuum, and we all echo her cry and gently clang our drinks together.

And then our voices and clanging are immediately drowned out by the siren shriek of the fire alarm.

"The sauce!" Dad calls out, rushing over to the smoking saucepan and dragging it off the hob.

Me and Clem spring into action, Clem yanking open the back door for air, me doing the same with the creaking, stiff window. Even Donna is helping, grabbing a tea towel and standing on tiptoes in her wedge shoes, all the better to flap smoke away from the squealing alarm in the kitchen ceiling.

A few frantic seconds later and everything is under control – apart from Dad, who is prawn pink and running the burning pan under the tap with one hand while rubbing his other hand across his head in consternation.

"How about we show Donna around while you make more sauce, Dad?" Clem suggests, taking both a deep breath and control of the situation at the same time. "Do you want to take her through to the living room first, Maisie?"

"Sure," I pant, while ushering Dad's slightly breathless girlfriend to follow me.

As we go out into the hall, I glance back and see Clem whipping a jar of Tesco pasta sauce from a cupboard and shoving it into Dad's hand. She really has gone up in my estimation in the last three minutes. . .

"It's very cosy," Donna says, gazing around the living room, running a hand over the top of the squashy sofa. Her dimples are showing again, and now I have the chance to study her properly, I realize that she's quite a bit younger than Dad.

I'm not great at estimating ages, but I reckon she's maybe about thirty, making Dad twelve years older.

Is that weird to think about? Or any more weird than thinking she might end up being our stepmum one day, if things work out?

"Do you want to see our rooms?" says Clem, appearing in the doorway.

"Well, only if you don't mind," Donna answers, not wanting to impose, I guess.

"Only if you don't mind that they're not all that tidy," Clem comes right back, leading the way up the stairs.

"Speak for yourself!" I say, feeling relaxed enough

now to try a little banter with my sister.

"The way *I* see it, what's the point in tidying when it's so disgusting to begin with?" Clem quips, reaching the landing and pushing her bedroom door open. "I promise you, Donna, what's on the floor in here will give you a *migraine*. . ."

"Oh dear, I see what you mean!" Donna laughs, glancing down at the swirls and whirls of Clem's carpet. "It *is* a bit . . . prehistoric!"

Clem suddenly does something *else* I can't remember ever happening: she bursts out laughing. Her face has lit up at Donna's funny and sympathetic remark, and immediately I know this is going to be OK. Clem thinks she's going to like this woman. And since Dad already likes her (loves her?) I can't help but feel a thrill.

Any hiccups going on between Dad and Donna? They're over.

We're all going to be all right.

This might be easier than any of us could've hoped for.

"So where do you live, Donna? Dad tells us nothing!" Clem chats away, closing the door to her room as I open the door to mine.

"I'm *way* on the other side of town," says Donna.

"Near the country park. We moved there when I was little and I didn't stray too far after that, I guess."

"So you don't know this area, then?" I add chattily, coming out with the most bland comment, I know, but it's just 'cause I'm trying to sound as friendly and easy-going as my sister.

But Donna seems to pause momentarily, like those fraction-of-a-seconds when DVDs freeze halfway through.

What?

What happened?

Did I say something to upset her?

"I–I haven't been round here for years," she finally says, a catch in her voice.

I'm slightly thrown, and shoot a quick look at Clem. Her eyes meet mine, and I spot the faintest hint of a frown. No one else would've made it out; only a sister. So she noticed that weird pause too?

"Those are all my favourite books," I chatter, hoping to smooth over the odd blip by pointing to the slightly squint shelf Dad put up over my desk earlier in the week.

"I *love* books," murmurs Donna, tilting her head sideways to read the spines, seeming normal and pleasantly ordinary once again.

"Stolen any of those from *me*, Maisie?" Clem asks, but for a change *doesn't* add her usual dollop of sarkiness to the top of those words.

"Um, nope – I've got much better taste in stories than *you* ever did," I say, risking a joke while I take a moment to grab Mum's photo from my chest of drawers and slip it inside her notepad. (Don't want Donna to see that right now; too strange.)

As for the notebook – I slip *that* under the decorated box I keep hair clips and bands in. (Don't know if Clem would feel weird seeing it, but I don't want to take *that* risk either.)

"And this, well, this is my view!" I carry on, walking over to the window, kicking the bottom of one of my overlong curtains out of the way. "Though it's not exactly exciting."

Donna turns from the bookshelf and looks past me out of the window.

Uh-oh.

Something is wrong.

"Not great, is it?" I try joking, attempting my brightest smile again.

This time, it doesn't work.

'Cause Donna is stepping closer to the window.

She's gone paler than pale.

Like she's seen a ghost. . .

No, no, *no*!

Has Kat appeared at the art room window?

I flip around in a panic – and see nothing.

Just a big, looming red-brick building, clouds buffeting across the rooftops, windows empty of life, dead or alive.

My immediate reaction is to reach out to Donna, to touch her arm, ask if she's all right – but I've only known her for about ten minutes, and it seems too much, too personal.

Instead I look beyond her traumatized expression, the pain in her eyes, and reach out – in words, at least – for my sister.

"*Clem*," I say urgently. "Help me!"

She turns from my books – just in time to see my curtains suddenly billowing.

And Donna swaying, staggering, fainting. . .

17

Enjoy life. Enjoy every strange and unexpected twist and turn.

Look, I *get* most of the advice that Mum wrote in her notebook, I really do.

But not all of it.

That one where she says, *Enjoy life. Enjoy every strange and unexpected twist and turn.*

How could she have written that, knowing a strange and unexpected twist or turn had landed her with an illness she'd never recover from?

But that's way back in the past, I suppose.

Here and now, I'm not enjoying this *particular* strange and unexpected twist or turn.

Donna is sitting next to Dad on the sofa, crying her eyes out.

This getting-to-know-you visit with our *maybe* future stepmum isn't exactly going great.

To be honest, I'm scared – properly scared.

To have her faint at my feet was one thing; to see her wordlessly sobbing now is another; but that look on her face at the window – I can't get it out of my head.

"Donna, please, *please* tell me what's wrong!" says Dad, holding her tight, stroking the damp hair from her face.

"Here," says Clem, handing Donna a glass of water with ice cubes in it.

She doesn't seem to notice, so Dad takes it instead.

"Thanks," he mouths at my sister.

"Should I call an ambulance? Maybe she hurt her head," Clem suggests.

"N–no, I don't need an ambulance," Donna manages to mutter, through her grief and tears and the soggy tissue covering her face.

Meanwhile, *I'm* perched here on the edge of the coffee table like a frightened little kid, not knowing what to say, think, do.

But spotting the dangling scrap of white paper in Dad's girlfriend's hand, I scrabble for the box of tissues next to me on the table.

"Here," I say, falling on to my knees in front of Donna, presenting her with the Kleenex.

She doesn't notice; her eyes are squeezed shut,

her breath raspy and hiccuping with sobs.

I'm thinking about placing the box gently on her lap when a sudden coolness swoops through me.

A tiny flash of a memory hits me: scents of flowers from the garden, plucked petals on my jeans. Kat there in front of me as the truth dawned about who she was, *what* she was.

My heart was racing, my head hurt . . . till Kat placed her hands on my knees, and I felt that soothing surge of a soft breeze brush over me, calming me.

Is she here?

Now?

I glance around – there's no one in the living room except me, Clem, Dad and Donna.

But I'm sure she *is* here, somehow.

Out of the corner of my eye, I sense a slight haze just in front of me, though I know if I blink it'll be gone.

A shift.

That's what it is.

Her.

It's enough for me to understand and to use the unexpected coolness in me, in my fingertips, to reach out to Donna.

I softly rest my hands palms down on her knees . . . and it happens.

She takes a halting, gathering breath, and her shoulders relax; her eyes blink away the last of her tears.

"Donna?" says Dad, relieved to see the change in her. "Can you tell us what's wrong?"

She nods. She gulps. She's definitely better but it still takes her a few minutes to collect herself enough to talk, so I keep my borrowed, healing hands right where they are.

"I didn't want to come here today. I mean, I didn't *ever* want to come here," Donna finally says, and Dad looks instantly crestfallen. "And not because of you, Jack – *or* your girls!"

Donna is staring at him, mascara smeared down her face, willing him to understand.

"What do you mean?" says Dad, struggling to make sense of what Donna's telling him.

"This place . . . the school. It has really, *really* bad memories for me."

"But you said you grew up near the country park," Clem butts in. "You didn't go to school here, did you?"

"No," says Donna, with a shake of her head.

"But my mother was head of the art department at Nightingale, and we lived a couple of streets away; I don't remember the name of the road, I was too young at the time. My big sister . . . *she* was a Nightingale girl."

The coolness in me swooshes around, turning slightly icy.

"Did something happen, Donna?" Dad asks, gently encouraging her.

"My sister stayed after school every day – she was in lots of clubs and did sports. Then when our mother finished work, they'd walk home together and collect me from my childminder on the way."

None of us says anything. All of us breathe as quietly as we can, so we don't disturb Donna, lost in her story.

"But every Friday, as a treat, the childminder would drop me off at the school at three-thirty, and me and my sister would paint and draw and scribble till Mum finished tidying up. It was lovely. *Lovely*."

The icy whirls inside me are giving me the shivers.

"But then there was the accident . . . it just felt so, *so* real again, seeing the school, the art room, and the roof terrace out of your window, Maisie!"

Donna is crying again, but slow, steady streams of tears instead of the hiccuping sobs of a few minutes ago.

"What happened?" I can't help push her, as the ice speeds up and down my back, races round and round my chest.

This might be it.

The final piece of Kat's puzzle.

"We lost her," Donna answers simply, broken-heartedly. "She went out on to the roof terrace, but no one knew why; my sister would've known that wasn't allowed. And no one saw – Mum only realized when she heard her scream, when she saw the open window. . ."

"Oh, no!" Dad gasps.

"Omigod," mumbles Clem.

But I'm holding it together; I have to know as much as there is to know.

"Katherine . . . she fell over the parapet?" I check.

"Yes," Donna nods, twisting the damp tissue into knots in her hand. "The school caretaker was first to get to her, but she was gone . . . gone. She was only thirteen."

Dad quickly passes the undrunk glass of water

over to Clem, and now wraps his *other* arm around Donna, slowly rocking her as she sinks gratefully into him.

Clem drops her head, bites her lip hard, lost for words.

Me?

I lay my head on Donna's lap, since Kat wants me to.

Same as I know she likes it very, *very* much when Donna lays a shaky hand on my hair and strokes it a few moments later.

And now the iciness is fading.

Kat's ebbing away from me.

I hope she's OK.

And in the sadness and muddle of the moment, I hope neither Clem, Dad or Donna realize I used Katherine's name without being told what it was.

"Can I make a suggestion?" Dad suddenly asks Donna. "It's going to sound mad, but it might help."

I think I know what he's going to ask her to do.

Pushing myself up on to my feet, I get ready to rush to the cupboard in the kitchen where Dad keeps his giant set of keys, if Donna answers yes. . .

18

Sometimes things never quite make sense; you just have to accept that.

"Maisie! MAISIE!"

It's friendly, but it's a shout that makes me stop in my tracks.

You don't ignore a friendly shout from your teacher, even when you *are* nearly home. (Even when home is only seventy-five steps across the playground and you're on step sixty-nine.)

I turn around and see Mrs Watson waving.

Patience is at her side.

I turn and walk back, wondering what's up.

Is Mrs Watson going to make a joke again about how distracted I was in registration this morning? "Hope your daydream is interesting, Miss Mills?" Mrs Watson teased when I didn't notice her calling my name only a few feet away from me.

I could hardly tell her I was lost in thoughts of yesterday evening's strange and unexpected twists and turns.

Lost in thoughts of Donna's sad story, of Kat's sad story.

Of words that helped in Mum's notebook: *Sometimes things never quite make sense; you just have to accept that.*

Those helped 'cause while it seemed like I'd found an ending to my friend's story, it still felt like a piece of the puzzle was lost somewhere, brushed under a carpet, chucked in a corner of the past where we'd never find it, Kat and me.

And like Mum wrote – all those years ago – we're just going to have to accept that.

Unless Kat can remember what Katherine was doing out on the roof terrace. . .

I need her to reappear. We need to talk.

"Yes, Mrs Watson?" I call out to my teacher now, squashing thoughts of Kat to the back of my mind for a brief moment.

"I've been trying to catch you between classes, but you're an elusive girl!" she says with a wide smile.

Not as elusive as Kat; every chance I got today I've been hurrying down dim and distant corridors, trying to glimpse her, even just a hint of her.

"Anyway, I was chatting to Miss Carrera in the staffroom at lunchtime," Mrs Watson carries on, regardless of my lack of explanation, "and she's keen on spring cleaning the art room. Lots of the older art projects are getting a bit worn and torn and have been there since *long* before she started."

How funny.

What would Miss Carrera and Mrs Watson think if they knew that Donna's fingers brushed past the junk sculpture last night, sending spirals of dust into the evening air? Would they report Dad to the head teacher for breaking the rules and doing his girlfriend a kindness at the same time? ("Thanks," we'd heard Donna say as she and Dad walked hand in hand across the playground after we'd taken the saddest walk down memory lane I can think of. "I think I needed to banish those demons. . .")

"So, I volunteered your services, Maisie!" Mrs Watson announces cheerfully. "Yours and Patience's."

I can see where this is going.

I can see Patience's still face, her dark-brown eyes scanning me, wondering what I'll make of this friendship matchmaking that Mrs Watson's just sprung on us. (I'm *sure* that's what it is.)

"You two are *just* the ultra-keen helpers she needs. Starting tomorrow, you'll grab a sandwich from the dining hall at lunchtime and take it up to her room, ready to start. All right?"

It doesn't matter how keen on this idea Mrs Watson is, Patience is hardly going to want to be forced into spending time with me. Is she?

"Yes, miss!" says Patience, smiling up at our teacher, and then surprising me by continuing the smile, only in my direction.

It must be an act, in front of Mrs Watson.

She doesn't really talk to me in class, so why would she—

Oh.

Behind Mrs Watson's shoulder; against the slight darkness of the entrance through the double doors.

A shift.

A shimmer.

A glimmer of a girl.

She's coming back to me.

"That's great," I hurriedly say to Mrs Watson, flashing a quick smile back at Patience while I'm at it. "But I'd better go now – I have this . . . thing."

I turn and half-walk, half-run towards the side door of our cottage, knowing she'll be following me, even be *ahead* of me.

"Kat?" I call out, as soon as the door thunks closed at my back.

I'm safe to shout, knowing that it'll be another hour at least till Clem saunters home. And Dad is busy round the school, whistling with happiness, I'll bet, after the watershed of last night.

Kat's not in the kitchen.

Not in the living room.

Not in my bedroom.

Not in – oh!

"What?!" Clem frowns at me from the floor of her room, where she's kneeling. She has a knife in her hand.

"I didn't think you'd be home," I tell her.

"I cut the last lesson. Don't tell Dad," she says, then gleefully sticks the knife in her hideous carpet and drags it through with an ominous tearing noise.

"What are you doing?" I ask, shocked at her vandalism, even if it is the ugliest piece of floor covering in the world.

"It's OK; Dad said I could. Donna told him we should get rid of it and paint the floorboards white, like she's done in her flat. God, I love that woman!"

"When did that happen?" I ask, thinking back to the conversation we'd had over tea, all huddled around the table in the glow of candles.

"After you went to bed, sleepyhead!" She looks up from her work and grins at me.

Of course I don't tell Clem the truth. I didn't head for bed last night because I was tired; I just wanted to watch the school from my room, to see if Kat was at her long window . . . but there was no sign, or shift, of her.

"Anyway, go – you're distracting me!" Clem orders, and I quickly pull her door shut.

And then, as I stand on the airless landing, I smell lavender . . . roses . . . cut grass . . . damp earth. . .

I know where she is.

"Are you all right?" I ask, stepping out into the brightness of the back garden and seeing her there, sitting waiting for me in the summerhouse.

"I'm OK, thanks," she smiles, but her face is thin, and her head leans against the one of the glassless window frames, as if she hasn't the energy to hold it up on her own.

"You heard it all last night?" I check with her, as I carefully avoid the encroaching stinging nettles and splintered wood in the summerhouse.

"Mm," she murmurs, seeming exhausted but happy. "And it was so lovely to meet her."

"To 'meet' her? That's a funny thing to say – Donna's your sister!" I say, taking a seat opposite.

"Hey, don't forget; *my* Donna was *that* size," Kat laughs, holding her hand out to toddler height. "My little star. I used to breathe on windows and draw these little stick figures of her. She loved it!"

"You did that in my room the first time you came, remember?" I say, thinking too of the matching stick figures on the inside of the art room window.

"Did I?" Kat says dreamily.

Her memory really does come in flashes and snatches, drifting back and forth in time.

"Kat, can you picture that day? Can you try really hard to think what happened to you before you fell?" I urge her, sensing that she's tired but I'm desperate to see if her mind can reach out and grab a wisp of an answer.

Kat closes her eyes tight, slaps her hands over her face, tries so hard to concentrate.

I hold my breath, rigid with hope.

Then she shakes her head, her bow flapping, her fingers falling away from her face.

"It's just sun and clouds and Donna's giggles – and then nothing."

"Oh, Kat. . ." I sigh sorrowfully.

My automatic reaction is to get up, go over and hug her, but before I do a shout jolts through me, anchoring me where I am.

"Maisie! MAISIE!"

It's the second time I've been shouted at, but this time it sounds more urgent than friendly.

"You've got to look at this!" Clem calls, hurrying towards me, her normally perfect hair bundled in a ponytail, messy carpet fibres coating her black leggings.

She's holding some folded paper in her hand.

"Climb through," I tell her, as she struggles to open the door to the summerhouse and fails.

"Pile of old rubbish," she mutters, hopping awkwardly in to join me and Kat.

Though she doesn't seem to have acknowledged Kat's there.

I glance over at my friend as my sister settles herself on the built-in wooden seat. Kat looks hazy to me, as if I have a filmy veil covering my eyes. She's smiling softly and shaking her head, touching a finger to her lips, letting me know Clem can't see her.

"What's up?" I ask, knowing that whatever it is, it has something to do with the flat folds of yellowed paper Clem's carrying.

"I found *this* under my carpet," she tells me, holding up what I now recognize as a newspaper. The local newspaper, going by the title.

"What's that doing under your carpet?" I wonder, confused.

"Before underlay was invented, people used to use old newspapers to line the floors, then put the new carpet down on top," Clem explains wearily, annoyed at having to give me a social history lesson. "But that's not the point."

"The point is. . .?" I try.

"Read the date," orders Clem, her navy-varnished nail tapping at a line of small text near the top of the page.

"May fifteenth, nineteen eighty-seven," I mutter, then the surprise sets in. "Has this got something to do with Donna's sister?"

"It's got *everything* to do with Donna's sister. Look!"

With a rustle and a smooth of Clem's hand, I find myself staring down at a front-page story.

There's a photo – taken with something like a fish-eye lens – of the Nightingale School playground. There are girls standing in huddles crying, or bending down to lay flowers near the main front doors.

My heart is racing and my eyes are blurring with tears; I'm not sure I can actually read what's written below it. Then I feel the cool rush as her hand rests on my shoulder, and I realize Kat is now standing beside me, leaning over to read her own story.

The coolness helps a little, but I'm still too flustered, too freaked to look directly at those harsh black words and the truth they tell.

I need to hear it from someone I love.

"I can't do this," I tell Clem. "Please just tell me what it says?"

I half expect Clem to bark at me to read it for myself, but she doesn't.

"The little girl – Donna, I mean – she snuck out on to the roof terrace when no one was looking," says Clem, her eyes skimming the article for me. "Her big sister Katherine saw her and rushed out after her. But Katherine was wearing her mum's long art apron over her school uniform, and as she rushed to grab her sister, she tripped on it."

"And fell over the parapet," I finish, visualizing the flapping white of the apron I saw trailing out of the art room window.

The stories of the whimsical Victorian ghost in her white petticoats . . . it was a fun, full-of-life girl called Katherine Mary Jessop the whole time. A girl who sang along to hits from 1987 as she helped her kid sister daub blobby buses and cars and people on sheets of paper while their mother pottered about, tidying and sorting her department. A girl who didn't want to get paint all over her uniform and so grabbed the nearest thing at hand. A simple piece of well-used cotton fabric that would trip her and trick her into leaving her world behind.

I'm supposed to be looking after her, I hear a faint whisper in my ear. *Mum's trusting me to look after her. If anything happens to Donna, I'm NOT going to be Mum's favourite person!*

"It was an *accident*," I say so loudly and clearly that it makes Clem jump.

"Well, yeah," she replies, unaware that I'm not saying that for *her* benefit.

"Accidents can be horrible, but they happen. And Katherine saved her sister. She *saved* her, so no one could be angry with her for that!"

"Well, duh, *no*," says Clem, staring at me as if I've gone slightly insane.

But I'll live with insane.

All that matters is that the puzzle is done, the last, lost piece pressed into position, for Katherine's sake.

As the touch of her cool fingers leaves my shoulder, I feel but don't see her go.

Till next time, I say silently to myself, hoping there will be one. . .

Epilogue Miss me, but not too much.

There never was a next time.

Just blank school windows, an empty summerhouse, long corridors with laughing, living girls.

In the long summer holidays, I'd wander the playgrounds with Dad, helping him water the shrubs and plants, bringing him coffee as he mowed the ever-growing lawn, hoping, fingers crossed, that I might somewhere and at some random moment see a shift . . . but there was nothing.

Nothing.

"Thank you *so* much for this. I really appreciate it," I hear Donna say, standing up after stroking the simple silver plaque that reads *In memory of Katherine Mary Jessop, Nightingale School student, much missed.*

The plaque is on a wooden stand at the bottom of a newly planted cherry blossom tree in the corner of the playground.

It's autumn now, so we'll have to watch this year's leaves fall first before the new shoots come next spring, followed by the fat puffs of pink flowers.

"The head teacher was just really glad we could do something to commemorate your sister," says Mrs Watson, who's here as a representative of the school, along with Miss Carrera, and Mahalia and June from the office, who all keep dabbing at their eyes. "And of course it was Jack who came to us to suggest it."

"Of course," says Donna, leaning into Dad, stretching up to kiss his cheek.

And it was Dad's idea never to tell Donna the newly discovered details of the accident in the first place.

"Her mother – her whole family – must have decided to keep it from her," he'd reasoned with me and Clem, the day we showed him the newspaper article. "Can you imagine what a burden that would be, to know that you – however innocently – were the cause of a tragedy like that?"

So Dad and Donna, me and Clem, the staff from

school; we're here just to celebrate and remember Katherine, nothing more.

And it's a pretty beautiful, pretty special moment.

Above us, the September sky is blue as blue can be, not a cloud troubling it.

Close by, children's laughter bubbles over the high red-brick wall that separates the school grounds from the neighbouring housing estate.

Clem is holding my hand, which feels very, very nice, but – and Mum would be proud of this – she has been very, very nice to me in general, ever since the we found out the truth about Katherine.

The night that happened, I had this sudden need for Clem to be the beloved big sister she once was. So at bedtime, I took a deep breath and tiptoed through to her room with Mum's notebook clutched hopefully to my chest. We ended up cuddled under her duvet, flicking through every single page together, taking turns to read out what Mum had written, chatting about what she meant.

"What do you think of this one?" I'd asked her, stopping at the very last page. "*Miss me, but not too much. . .*"

"She's just telling us to be happy, to get on with our lives," Clem said simply.

And since that bit of Clem-and-me time, it's been great between us. I mean, we haven't gone back to the pretending-to-be-dogs or tickle-fighting games of our childhood, and she still nags me if I drink the last of the orange juice or stay in the shower too long. (And *boy*, did she tell me off for writing that pretentious and dramatic *R.I.P. my life* stuff at the back of the notebook. . .) But like I say, it's more or less great, which is, I guess, great.

"Would you like to come back to the house. . .?" Dad offers the teachers, and Mahalia and June.

"No, no, we don't want to intrude," they all say, practically in unison.

Maybe Mrs Watson and the others assume we're all going to be very sombre, but we're not. Dad has made Mexican food for tea, and me and Clem put together a playlist of songs from 1987.

The staff might picture us sitting stiffly around the kitchen table this evening, but actually, we're planning to salsa around it to "La Bamba" – and "La Isla Bonita" by Madonna; Dad remembered that was one of Mum's teenage favourites.

Patience has promised to come along later, so it'll be quite a little party.

Me and Patience? We became best friends while

we helped Miss Carrera all those lunchtimes in the art room last term. She was really touched by Katherine's story (though I never told her about *Kat*).

It's kind of funny; Dad goes over the top whenever Patience comes around, cracking endless bad jokes and forcing cookies on her. I think he panicked a bit when I told him me and Kat had "drifted apart", and wants to bribe Patience into staying as my long-term friend. . .

"Are you sure?" Dad tries to persuade the retreating school staff. "You'd be most welcome!"

"Thanks, but we'd all better be going; leave you to it," says Mrs Watson, heading off across the playground, which was deserted by home-streaming students an hour or so ago.

Miss Carrera, Mahalia and June follow her, while Dad and Donna call out their thanks again, then lead the way towards the cottage.

"Coming?" says Clem, tugging gently at my hand.

"In a minute," I tell her.

She nods, smiles, and strolls off after Dad and Donna.

As soon as I'm alone, I feel for the scrap of paper in my pocket.

Taking it out, I stare at the drawing I doodled

earlier: the outline of a squashy star, inside it a bigger stick figure holding hands with a diddy little one.

"I'll miss you, Kat, but hopefully not *too* much," I whisper, tucking the tiny drawing into the grass in front of the plaque.

Mum's right; everyone has to move on.

Not so long ago I searched – and I found – the girl who wasn't there.

But now there are girls who *are* here, girls like Patience and Natasha and the others who all want to know me. Who *never*, by the way, had any idea about the bad stuff that happened at my old school. They only ever stayed away from me because I was making such a point of staying away from *them*. . .

Smiling at my own stupidity, I straighten up – then tune in again to the giggles of children playing on the other side of the perimeter wall.

Or . . . or *is* it coming from that direction?

A waft of a breeze seems to guide my gaze, to gently turn my face towards the school building.

Is *that* where it's coming from?

The art room?

The three long windows. . .

I guess the movement I can see could simply be

the reflection of the sun, or a passing plane, but I know it's not.

It's a shift; an echo through time of two sisters – one big, one small – fooling around, playing while their mum looks on.

The bigger of the two stops suddenly.

She looks my way.

Puts her hand on the window, then waves her funny, dumb little-kid wave.

"Hi. . ." I croak, madly waving back.

But I really mean bye.

Because Kat has already faded away, along with the laughter.

This time, deep down, I know she's a girl who really isn't here any more. . .